THE SCHOOL FOR

WICKED WITCHES

WILL TAYLOR

THE SCHOOL FOR
WICKED
Witches

WILL TAYLOR

SCHOLASTIC

Copyright © 2024 by Will Taylor

All rights reserved. Published by Scholastic Inc., *Publishers since 1920*. SCHOLASTIC and associated logos are trademarks and/or registered trademarks of Scholastic Inc.

The publisher does not have any control over and does not assume any responsibility for author or third-party websites or their content.

No part of this publication may be reproduced, stored in a retrieval system, or transmitted in any form or by any means, electronic, mechanical, photocopying, recording, or otherwise, without written permission of the publisher. For information regarding permission, write to Scholastic Inc., Attention: Permissions Department, 557 Broadway, New York, NY 10012.

This book is a work of fiction. Names, characters, places, and incidents are either the product of the author's imagination or are used fictitiously, and any resemblance to actual persons, living or dead, business establishments, events, or locales is entirely coincidental.

ISBN 978-1-339-04267-1

10 9 8 7 6 5 4 3 2 1   24 25 26 27 28

Printed in the U.S.A.   40

First printing 2024

Book design by Maeve Norton

FOR THE KIDS WHO DON'T FIT IN.
YOU'RE AWESOME.

1

THE FIRST DAY

Ava Heartstraw stared around her at the sparkling great hall of West Oz Witch Academy, feeling very, very nervous.

She'd been feeling this way since before dawn, when she'd left her family's brick moss farm on the edge of the Impassable Desert and set off in a neighbor's cart for Muzzlewump, the nearest town. Muzzlewump was small by most people's standards, but enormous to Ava, who had never been so far from home in all her eleven-and-a-quarter years.

The neighbor had dropped Ava off at the train station, leaving her to find a seat on the express alone, biting her lip and staring out the window as the great machine thundered to life, taking her farther and farther away from her home, her parents, her eleven older sisters and brothers, and her miniature pet tortoise, Peaches.

Ava hated crying—it made her nose all runny—so she'd kept her spirits up by remembering her family's excitement when the official messenger parrot had arrived three days before. The parrot had announced that the Witch Council of Oz had detected magic in Ava and demanded her presence at West Oz Witch Academy for training—an enormous honor. The parrot had also demanded a cup of strawberry iced tea, but since the poor family didn't have any strawberries, or ice, or tea, it left disappointed. All that might change once Ava graduated, though. She would be an important and powerful person, able to help her family.

Ava's family had always been poor, but that was just how things were when you farmed brick moss on the edge of the Impassable Desert. Tending brick moss was hard work, even with so many hands to help, and while her parents tried to keep a cheerful face on things, Ava had heard them whispering at night about their worries for the future. Worst of all, she was still too young to help with the really difficult work. Sometimes, when she was feeling really low, she wondered if she was only getting in the way.

Ava's brightest goal, the thing that kept back her tears the whole lonely train ride, was the image of her triumphant return. She pictured all the wonderful ways she could make her family's lives easier once she became a witch, from healing sore backs to keeping the well full to adding extra rooms to the house so she and her eleven sisters and brothers wouldn't have to sleep piled up like sand lizards on the scratchy kitchen floor.

Finally, the express had slowed to a stop, and Ava

found herself on the platform beside a tall, imposing woman in silver robes, along with half a dozen other kids from the train.

If Ava had been impressed by Muzzlewump, she was speechless as their little group marched through the high gates of West Oz Witch Academy. The school was a shining silver dome with a glimmering lacework of windows, balconies, and crystal ornaments. Ava had never even imagined a building so beautiful. What must the rest of Oz be like if this was what magic could do?

The imposing woman had introduced herself as Madame Lilac and led them into a grand hall at the heart of the school. There were clear crystal columns, rows of marble benches rising on either side, a platform with two throne-like chairs in front, and a ceiling fitted with shining lamps shaped like stars. Most impressive of all to Ava, flowering plants grew everywhere. Vines twined up the walls trailing bell-shaped flowers in pinks, purples, blues, and creams. The platform with the thrones was carpeted with flowering moss. And tall, delicate windows set along the far wall showed the school gardens bursting and shimmering with more plants than Ava had ever dreamed of.

The new students were told to wait, then left alone. Ava tilted back her head and stared.

"Psst," hissed a girl's voice. Ava turned.

The girl beckoning to her was a little taller than Ava and had pale skin, lots of curly blond hair, and a thick gold necklace. A cluster of other girls stood around her, all in matching yellow overalls.

Ava smiled, feeling a happy sort of nervousness now. Was she about to make her first school friends?

"Hey," the blond girl said as Ava joined them. "Okay, so we were just wondering: Um, what exactly are you wearing?"

The whole group fought to suppress giggles as Ava felt her happiness drain away. She looked down at her clothes.

Ava had put on her very best that morning: a dress made of brown burlap over linen, embroidered with a pattern of green cactuses. It had been a special present for her eleventh birthday, and it was the only thing she owned that was not a hand-me-down from her sisters and brothers. Her father had worked on it for months in secret. She loved the way it looked against her sand-colored skin and wavy brown hair.

"I'm wearing this," Ava said, clenching her hands in the burlap. "It's my favorite dress."

"If you say so." The blond girl grinned. "What's with the cactuses, then? Does your family farm sand or something?"

Ava felt flustered. Why was this girl asking these questions? Why wouldn't the rest of them stop giggling?

"My family grows brick moss," she answered. "Out on the edge of the Impassable Desert. It's a really important job. Brick moss makes the strongest bricks in the world."

"Oh wow, bricks! That sounds so, *so* awesome!" The girl snorted. "Seriously, though, who would want to live in a desert? I'm pretty sure all normal people live in towns."

Ava thought of the desert, of the painted sunsets, the friendly miniature tortoises, the magnificent stars at night. Sure, the days were scorching and the nights were freezing, and most of the plants were sharp, but there were probably difficulties like that no matter where you lived. The desert was her home. Her family lived there. That was enough for her to love it.

"I would want to live there," Ava said, trying to sound as certain as she felt. It was hard with all these girls looking at her. "It's beautiful."

"Yeah, okay." The blond girl tilted her head. "What do you think your magic will turn out to be, then? *Sunburn protection?*"

The whole group guffawed, and Ava felt her face get hot. She did not like this girl. Not one bit.

Besides, Ava already knew what her magic was. The beginnings of it, at least. She had discovered it by accident out in the desert. But she certainly wasn't going to tell *this* girl about it.

"My magic's my business," she said. "What about yours?"

The girl's smile widened. "Don't worry, Little Miss Cactus. You'll see."

There was a muffled boom, and Ava and the girls stepped apart as a door in the far corner of the hall opened. A stream of older kids walked in, all wearing perfectly tailored silver uniforms. They did not acknowledge the newcomers but marched in neat rows up the steps and onto the marble benches.

Ava returned to where she'd been standing, glad to be done talking to the mean girl. She couldn't hold back a guilty little sigh as she watched the older kids, though. She really did love the dress her father had made, but it was going to be wonderful to be one of these proud-looking students in their silky silver jackets and ties. She pictured visiting home and all her siblings admiring her gorgeous uniform as she told them stories of her life as a witch out in the big, wide world.

At last the older students were seated, and an expectant silence settled over the hall.

Ava was just looking around, wondering who would be coming in next, when a crackle of sparkles lit up the platform, the scent of oranges shimmered through the room, and two people appeared out of nowhere in the waiting thrones.

The figure on the left was an old man with dark brown skin and absolutely no hair. His face was deeply lined and wrinkled, and Ava thought he looked kind. The old man wore a silver suit similar to the students' uniforms but much fancier, with tassels and trim and shining crystal buttons.

The figure on the right was a woman—Ava honestly couldn't say whether she was old or young—with rose-gold skin and a cloud of frizzy black hair. She wore tall, sky-blue boots and long silver robes so shiny they looked like liquid. She gave off an aura of command, power, and judgment. Ava instantly admired her.

The old man rose to his feet.

"Good day to you," he said, in a voice as wobbly as the air above hot sand. "My name is Professor Ploosh, director of students here at West Oz Witch Academy, and this"—he bowed to the woman seated beside him—"is Dean Waterwash, the head of our school. To our new students, greetings. The test to prove you are worthy to join our academy will begin momentarily. Pass the test, and you will be welcomed among us. Fail"—his smiling, wrinkled face became stern—"and you will be turned away this very hour and never set foot in these hallowed halls again!"

2

THE FIRST TEST

Ava gulped. A test? Already? But she hadn't had a chance to learn anything yet!

"Do not look so nervous," warbled Professor Ploosh. "This is merely to check whether your magic is good or wicked. And there should be nothing to worry about; the West hasn't produced a wicked witch in two hundred years. We have the best record of all the Witch Academies, North, South, East, and West. That's why when people meet a West Oz Witch, they say WOW!"

A murmur of proud agreement rippled through the hall.

"Form an orderly line, please, and we will call you forward one by one to demonstrate your magic for the school."

A short, pink-haired boy standing in front of Ava went as white as a cactus flower as the new students shuffled together. He turned and caught Ava's eye.

"I—I can't do magic in front of everyone," he whispered. "I've never done magic at all! The parrot must have made a mistake! I don't even think I'm a witch!"

"You'll be fine," Ava whispered back. The boy trembled, looking green around the edges.

Ava noticed the rude blond girl had pushed her way to the front, with her friends squeezed together behind her.

Professor Ploosh waved the girl forward, directing her to stand on a crystal star set into the floor.

"Name?" he asked.

"Sheridan Gracefeather Montstable-Jones," she said, her loud, snappy voice echoing around the hall.

"And have you performed magic yet?"

Sheridan tossed her hair. "I have."

"Very good. Do you require any tools to demonstrate your talents?"

"Hot chocolate, please."

Professor Ploosh waved his hand, and a silver mug appeared on the floor in front of Sheridan, brimming with chocolate.

"Begin when you are ready."

All the kids in line craned their necks to see as Sheridan picked up the mug and took a deep breath. Ava didn't like Sheridan, but she couldn't wait to see what would happen. Would she make the drink float? Grow marshmallows on top? Transform it to chocolate ice?

What Ava did not expect was for Sheridan to turn the

mug over and dump the dark, sticky contents all over her gorgeous, pristine clothes.

The whole hall gasped. Chocolate ran down Sheridan and glooped onto the floor.

Sheridan kept her cool. She took another deep breath, snapped her fingers, and with a sudden sizzle of energy the dark stain was gone.

Ava found herself clapping along with everyone else as Sheridan turned a circle with the mug—magically full again—held out for all to see.

"Excellent, excellent!" Dean Waterwash called. She had a deep, rich voice that soared above the noise like a desert eagle. "You clearly have very good magic and will make WOW Academy proud. Please take a seat with your new classmates."

Madame Lilac waved to Sheridan from a row of empty benches just beside the platform.

Ava felt a rush of relief. This first test was going to be easy! She just had to show the teachers what she could already do. Nothing to it.

Sheridan's friends went next, and while all of them passed, none of their performances were as dramatic as Sheridan's. Most had never done magic before, so Professor Ploosh provided objects for simple tests. One managed to make a book float a few inches above her palm. Another turned a red apple green. Another surrounded himself with a cloud of rainbow bubbles. And another filled a paper bag with the sound of falling rain. Ava was amazed at how many different kinds of magic there were. A whole new world was opening before her, and here she was, a part of it.

One by one the empty benches filled up, and soon there was only the pink-haired boy left in front of Ava.

"Oh no, oh no, oh no," he muttered as a round boy with poofy black hair made a pencil write glowing letters in the air. "I can't do this. But I can't fail!"

"What happens if someone *does* fail?" Ava whispered.

"If you really have no magic, I think they just send you home," the boy replied. "But if your magic shows any wickedness, you get sent to the School for Wicked Witches. I heard about it from my old South Oz pen pal. It's a school far, far away where they turn kids with wicked magic good. It's supposed to be a horrible place, with the strictest discipline, the meanest teachers, and the bitterest food in all of Oz. And the worst of it is you have to stay there until they think you're good enough, no matter how long that takes. Even if it's forever!"

Ava shuddered. Being sent to a school full of wicked students somewhere far, far away sounded like the very worst thing she could imagine. It was a relief to know her own magic was good.

"Next!"

The boy stepped forward, and Ava felt an excited squirm at being at the front of the line. She thought about her family and how proud they were going to be.

"Name?" called Professor Ploosh.

"H-Henry B-Buffle," the boy stammered.

"Proceed."

Ava watched as Henry tried his best with the various objects Professor Ploosh offered him. He tried to make a moth land on his nose—it went straight for the nearest star light. He tried to fix a broken ruler—it stayed snapped in two. When he couldn't manage to bend a candle flame, Dean Waterwash's face pinched into a frown. Over on the benches, Sheridan and her friends were openly laughing.

"Come on, Henry!" Ava whispered under her breath.

At last, Professor Ploosh threw a beach ball directly at Henry's head. Henry gave a little scream and ducked . . . and the moment he did, the ball stopped, reversed course, and flew back to the professor's hands.

Henry looked as surprised as Ploosh.

Dean Waterwash sat up in her chair. "Interesting!" she said. "Do it again."

Professor Ploosh threw the ball again, Henry ducked (without the scream this time), and the same thing happened. Then the professor and the dean tried it together.

For the next few minutes the pair of them threw beach balls, bouncy balls, eggs, coat hangers, and ceramic giraffes at Henry, and no matter what they magicked up, nothing made contact. When Henry Buffle ducked, things flew back where they came from. Every time.

At last Henry took his seat on the benches, looking dazed, and Ava was up. Her stomach fluttered as she lifted her chin, smoothed her burlap dress, and walked to the star.

"Name?"

"Ava Heartstraw."

Dean Waterwash peered down her nose. "Ah, yes, I heard you'd been summoned. The *desert* girl."

There was a hiss of whispers throughout the hall, and Ava felt her ears go hot. Why had Dean Waterwash put that twist on the word *desert*?

"And have you performed magic yet?" asked Professor Ploosh. He was beginning to sound bored with the question.

"Yes!" Ava couldn't resist shooting a glance at Sheridan, who arched one eyebrow and took a show-offy sip of her hot chocolate. Ava felt her jaw tighten. She would show her. She would show all of them what a girl from the desert could do. "Yes, I have."

"Very well. Do you need any tools to demonstrate?"

"A plant, please. The greener the better."

Professor Ploosh wiggled his ears, and a potted juicy-pop tree appeared beside her. Ava smiled. She couldn't *wait* until she could do that; her mother loved juicy-pop fruit.

Right now, though, it was time to focus.

Ava had discovered her magic while working with the brick moss back home. Brick moss grew slowly because it saved up all its water underground where the hot sun couldn't steal it. One day Ava had gotten a funny tingling in her hands, and she realized she could sense the water in the plant. With a little practice, she learned to move the water from one plant to another. She even taught herself how to pull the faint moisture deep in the sand and feed it to the moss. It only made a small difference, but it was still magic, and Ava was certain everyone could see it happen if she started with something green and leafy for a change. The more impressive she could make this—the more she could show up Sheridan—the better.

Facing the tree, Ava reached out for whatever watery energy it held—and gasped in shock. There was so much water here! *So much!* The air, the ground, the plants around her: Everything was surging with water. For a moment it was completely overwhelming, but she bit her lip, managed to wrap her mind around it all, and got to work on the tree.

First, she guided the juice out of the juicy-pop fruits and into the stems, leaving just enough behind to keep the plant upright.

Next, she nudged the liquid down into the roots. She could feel them growing down in the soil, doubling and tripling to make room for their new store of water. There was a loud crack as the pot shattered, the enormous roots spilling out.

Ava heard gasps from the crowd. She grinned. She was doing *great*. The juicy-pop tree had taken on the thin, veiny look of all sturdy desert plants, and the leaves had lost their insect-attracting green. Just a little longer and the whole tree would be perfectly camouflaged as a gnarled, twisted stump.

But would that be enough to impress Dean Waterwash? Enough to make Sheridan and her friends realize how wrong they'd been to make fun of her?

Ava closed her eyes and reached out even farther. She'd never tried anything like this before—she was making it up as she went—but the more she stretched her powers, the more water she found. She pulled every drop she could sense into the roots of her juicy-pop tree.

Her head swam as a roaring filled her ears. Lights

flashed in the darkness behind her eyelids. She felt as though she were falling into space, the way she sometimes did if she lay out on the dunes staring up into the stars. She felt giddy and powerful and a little scared. She felt amazing.

"Miss Heartstraw!" A thundering voice from the platform cracked through her, shattering her daze.

Ava opened her eyes. The roaring in her ears faded out. She looked around, and her breath caught in her throat.

The hall looked completely different.

The delicate flowering vines covering the walls were dead, their leaves brown and their blossoms shriveled into pale wisps. The dean's platform was covered in a burnt-orange crust of dead moss. The beautiful windows now looked out onto a crunchy, crackly wilderness of withered former gardens.

Along the benches, Sheridan was knocking desiccated chocolate powder out of her cup.

The girl who'd turned her apple green was holding a withered lump of fruit leather.

The boy once surrounded by rainbow bubbles was coated in a dry, iridescent film.

Wildest of all, the floor of the hall was filled with an enormous, tangled mass of juicy-pop roots. They throbbed with water, twisting together into gnarled, terrifying shapes like some nightmare monster from deep underground. The roots had even climbed up onto the benches, forcing the silver-robed students to huddle together to avoid being trapped or injured.

All around the hall, students and grown-ups alike were staring open-mouthed at Ava.

Dean Waterwash and Professor Ploosh were both on their feet, their faces like winter dust storms.

Ava gulped.

She'd gone too far.

Way too far.

"Sorry!" she said, her voice coming out high and squeaky in the shocked silence. "I'm sorry! I can fix this!"

She had no idea if this was true, but she hated the way everyone was looking at her. She hadn't *meant* to drain all the beautiful plants dry. She hadn't *meant* to create a hideous root monster. She hadn't meant to do anything wrong at all.

Professor Ploosh started to speak, raising a wrinkled hand, but Ava was already reaching back out for her power. The world disappeared again as she thought the situation through. If she'd made things go wrong by pulling all this water *out* of her surroundings, then maybe she could fix her mistake by sending it back.

She merged with the vast store of moisture trapped in

the roots, feeling it pressing on her mind as she tried to force it to do what she wanted. *Go back,* she thought with all her might. *Go back where you belong.*

But her magic seemed to have plans of its own, because the more she tried, the worse the pressure got. She thought she heard distant screaming, but it was taking everything she had just to keep her connection with her magic.

Then, all at once, the water seemed to give in. Ava felt a moment of giddy triumph . . .

. . . then she heard the explosion. The screams redoubled. A horrible smell hit her.

She opened her eyes.

For the rest of her life, Ava Heartstraw would never forget that first glimpse of the devastation she'd brought to the West Oz Witch Academy great hall.

The root monster had burst. Before it had, though, she'd apparently made it grow even larger, snaking over all the benches, storming up the marble columns, and coiling around students and teachers alike.

That meant when the explosion came, everyone in the hall was in the way. Chunks of root and thick, green, oily slime covered everything. The slime smelled like sweaty feet and sour milk. Dozens of students had been knocked to the ground. Madame Lilac was holding a twisted ankle.

Three of the beautiful star lights were lying in pieces on the floor. Half the windows looking out on the ruined gardens had shattered.

The only person in the whole hall not covered in slime was Ava. Gazing around at the total devastation, she began to laugh.

She felt awful about it, but there was nothing she could do. Laughing was just what she did when she got really, truly, extremely nervous. Some people got the shakes. Other people cried. Ava laughed.

She stood in the center of the chaos, cackling, waiting to see what would happen next.

She didn't have to wait long.

"Miss Heartstraw!" Dean Waterwash's deep voice shook as she magicked the slime from her face and robes. "What you have done today has brought shame upon these halls and all who study here." She drew herself up to her full height and raised a trembling finger. "I have no choice but to declare you and your magic . . . wicked!"

3

WICKED

Ava sat alone in Dean Waterwash's office in the upper curve of the dome, trying to stay calm.

Madame Lilac had rushed her out of the great hall amid an absolute frenzy from the other students, deposited her here, told her not to move, and left. Ten minutes later, Ava was still tapping nervously on the arms of an uncomfortable wooden chair, waiting to hear her fate.

Henry Buffle had said anyone with wicked magic got sent to the School for Wicked Witches. Ava shuddered at the thought. She did not want to go to the School for Wicked Witches. It sounded like a terrible place, and it wasn't like she belonged there.

. . . Right?

She couldn't believe what she'd just done in the great hall—so much mess and mayhem, other kids' magic ruined, people injured, and those poor plants! All because she was trying to show off and prove Sheridan wrong about her. The worst thing she'd ever done before today was break her mother's best moss-digging tool and let one of her brothers take the blame, and that had been nothing compared to this.

But was she wicked?

She shook her head. Of course not. She'd messed up pretty spectacularly, but that wasn't the same thing. You had to mean it to be wicked, didn't you? And wasn't the fact that she felt super awful proof that she was good?

But then, what had happened?

I have no choice but to declare you and your magic wicked—that was what Dean Waterwash had said. Could she have been partly right? Could there be something wrong with Ava's *magic*?

She remembered the humming in her ears, the dizzy feeling, the sense of power slipping out of her control.

Could her magic be wicked all on its own? Or—Ava swallowed hard—could it have turned bad because her reasons for wanting to be impressive secretly weren't all that nice?

They were both horrible thoughts.

Tears welled in the corners of her eyes, and she brushed them away angrily. She was *not* going to cry. She was *not* going to let Dean Waterwash or Professor Ploosh come in and see her with her nose running.

She tried distracting herself by looking around the office.

It was a beautiful room. The walls were painted dove

gray and hung with framed diplomas and paintings of lakes and mountains. A carved crystal chair stood behind a gleaming desk covered in neat piles of papers. There were ferns and orchids in silver pots; bookshelves lined with tomes and trophies; and a golden grandfather clock big enough for Ava to climb into with a lightning-bolt pendulum and an enormous, curly *W* perched at its top like a crown. The whole room was lit by a floor-to-ceiling stained-glass window showing a waterfall, filling the space with every shade of blue and white imaginable.

Ava gazed at the window, watching the colors change as a cloud drifted past the sun outside.

She gave a start as the door burst open.

Dean Waterwash swept into the room. She was clean again, though the smell of the slime hovered in the air. Her liquid-silver robes swirled as she marched over to stand behind the desk.

The dean did not sit down in the crystal chair, nor did she look at Ava. Instead, she closed her eyes, steepled her fingers in front of her pursed lips, and let out a long breath through her nose.

Ava waited, terrified.

"Do you know," Dean Waterwash said, her eyes still closed, "how long two hundred years is?"

Ava couldn't think of an answer.

"It is a very, *very* long time, Miss Heartstraw. Dean Phyllis Prancypants was running this academy the last time West Oz produced a wicked witch, and every leader of this school since, all nine of them—including me—have looked back on her term with scorn and shame. And now *you*." Her eyes flew open, and she stabbed a finger at Ava. "*You* have dared to bring your wickedness into my school and ruin everything! Now *my* name will go down in history alongside that of Dean Prancypants! Future deans will look down on *me*! And it's all"—she jabbed the air with each word—"your—fault!"

Ava cringed, but she clung to her courage. "I don't think I'm wicked!" she squeaked.

Dean Waterwash goggled at her, and Ava rushed ahead, hardly knowing what she was saying.

"It's just my magic, honest! There's too much water out here! If you let me stay, maybe I can learn to control it. Wouldn't that be good? Learning how to make wicked magic good again? You could tell everyone what I did was all a mistake, and—"

"Silence!" Dean Waterwash clacked her teeth, making a blast of freezing air billow through the room. "How dare you contradict me?" Her dark eyes pinned Ava to the chair. "You *are* wicked, little witch. Everyone in this school saw it with their own eyes. I will remember the sight of you cackling over your destruction as long as I live! I have personally come face-to-face with wickedness out there in the world, and I say you are as bad as Osmuth Rust, or Filbert the Cruel, or even Vivienne Morderay!"

Ava shivered. Tales of the few wicked witches loose across Oz had made their way out to the desert, but she'd never in a million years dreamed someone would be comparing them to her.

"And if I cannot escape my fate as the dean who broke a perfect two-hundred-year record," Dean Waterwash continued, "you *certainly* cannot escape yours. In any case, the Wicked Wagon is already on its way."

A blade of ice slipped down Ava's back.

"The w-wicked what?" she peeped.

The sunlight shining through the waterfall suddenly cut out as a huge shape flew past the window.

"The Wicked Wagon," said the dean. "The transport that carries bad children securely to the School for Wicked Witches, which is a fortress on an island in a lake of boiling water surrounded by hills made of broken glass. All of which is to say"—she curled one corner of her mouth— "once a child arrives at the fortress, there is no way out until she has been permanently cured of her wickedness."

Ava's insides flipped over. Henry Buffle's pen pal had been right! "H-how long does that take?" she gasped.

"The fastest rehabilitation on record," said Dean Waterwash, turning toward the window, "was seven years, ten months, and sixteen days."

Dean Waterwash wiggled her pinkies at the waterfall, making the stained glass melt away just as a massive wooden box floated into view outside.

It was a sinister-looking thing, all black and patchy gray, with iron wheels and a sideways door sealed with a heavy bolt. Ava could see a single window set with bars.

The box was hitched to a terrifying creature made entirely of dark blue stone. It had the head and torso of a man, the body of a wolf, and enormous batlike wings. Its human part was dressed in stone clothes, with a shirt and vest, a flat cap, and suspenders disappearing into the wolf fur.

The creature looked in through the window, bared its teeth, and winked.

"'Allo, Dean!" it said. "Never thought I'd be back 'ere! 'Aven't seen this place since Prancypants was in charge! Bet you wasn't 'spectin' to be chattin' to a gargoyle today, was ya?"

"Certainly not," snapped Dean Waterwash. "It's terrible to see you, Gern." She pointed to the locked wagon. "Are there any more wicked children in there?"

"Nah," said Gern. "Dropped off the wicked 'uns from

the North, East, an' South already, didn't I? You West lot always did test last, an' after all this time nobody 'spected to 'ear from yeh! I'm s'posed to be on me holidays!"

"How tragic for you. Well, if there are no dangerous children lurking inside . . ." She gestured impatiently, and Gern flapped his wings, bringing the wagon as close to the window as possible. A little more pinkie wiggling unlocked the door and sent it falling onto the windowsill like a plank.

Dean Waterwash turned to Ava. "In," she said, pointing at the box.

Ava leapt to her feet, gazing in horror at the dark opening. "N-no!" she yelped. "I want to go home!"

She made a desperate dash for the door, but a click of the dean's tongue brought Ava's chair to life. Long wooden fingers sprouted from its arms, and within seconds Ava was wrapped in its clutches and heading for the window.

"Help!" she screamed. She twisted and kicked, but the chair held her fast as it galloped onto the plank. She had one terrifying glimpse of the sloping silver wall, the empty air, and the ruined gardens down below before she was tumbled into the box.

The heavy door slammed into place, and as Ava staggered to her feet in the splintery darkness, she heard the crisp metal clank of the Wicked Wagon's lock sliding home.

4

THE WICKED WAGON

Ava lost her footing again as the Wicked Wagon lurched into the sky. She landed with a thump on a narrow wooden bench and hung on for dear life, her back pressed against the wall.

Up and up they flew, the wagon bouncing with each flap of Gern's great stone wings. Ava began to feel sick. Finally, the wagon leveled, the ride smoothed out, and she nervously opened her eyes.

A square of bright sunlight shone through the bars in the little window, just enough to see by. Ava wasn't so sure that was a good thing.

The inside of the Wicked Wagon was as horrible as its name. The walls, floor, and benches were made of dark, greasy-looking wood clamped together with iron. Splinters jabbed out everywhere. There was a suspicious stain in one corner. The air smelled like onions and sweat.

But the thing that made Ava's stomach flip over most were the carvings. Every inch of the Wicked Wagon was covered in scratched messages from previous passengers.

It was like being shouted at from all sides, and she couldn't stop herself from reading a few.

There's no way out!

I'm sorry Mom

Someone please feed my cat Gilly

Jasper was here

Helllllp!

They'll PAY for this

East Witches Forever!

Oats oats oats

Abandon all hope

I'll show them wicked!

Ava forced herself to stop reading. Getting carefully to her feet, she crossed to the door as the wagon vibrated under her, rocking slightly on the wind. There was no handle, so she aimed a kick at the ugly old thing, letting out her feelings. It stayed solidly shut.

Moving to the window, she noticed a smooth patch of wood under the bars. She rested her chin on it, looking out, then realized with a jolt that that must be exactly how the smooth patch got made. How many kids over how many years had done just what she was doing? How many hopeful, excited students like her had been plucked from their schools and unfairly carted off to the School for Wicked Witches?

Ava felt a prickle roll down her back as she realized it might not always be unfair. Some of the other students might actually be wicked—wicked on purpose. What if *all* the students were wicked and she was heading into a fortress full of bullies on *top* of cruel teachers, bitter food, and terrifying security?

She squinted out between the bars, her mind spinning.

They were high, high up, passing puffy white clouds in a perfect blue sky. Ava couldn't see much of the ground, but what she could see held fields and forests rolling by in more colors than she could name. Tears burned her eyes as she thought of her family and her simple desert home. Would it really be years before she saw them all again?

Time moved on. The land crawled below them, and the wagon swayed and rattled. Ava's spirits sank lower and lower as the patch of sun coming through the bars shifted against the wall.

Finally, she turned from the window, deciding she may as well try to rest on the narrow bench. As she did, a glint between two of the floorboards caught her eye.

She knelt and dug out a short pin topped with a square of topaz.

It looked old. How long had it been there, waiting for some fresh victim of the Wicked Wagon to find it? The thought made her shiver again, but the pin gave her a tiny spark of hope. Topaz was her mother's favorite. She tucked the pin in the pocket of her dress and lay down on the bench. Someday, she decided, she would give it to her mother as a present. Someday *soon*.

She lay on the bench with her eyes closed, listening to the wind, going over the facts of her predicament:

It had been a genuine accident, but she'd really messed up big-time at WOW Academy.

She wasn't wicked, but apparently her water magic could be if she tapped into it for the wrong reasons.

She was on her way to the School for Wicked Witches, and there was nothing she could do to change that.

All she *could* do, then, was decide what to do once she got there. Maybe if she explained the situation they would let her go back home? Maybe there would be a wicked-ness test she could deliberately fail?

Whatever happened, she decided, she absolutely would *not* be repeating the scene she'd caused at WOW Academy. There was too much danger of accidentally proving the grown-ups right, so she wasn't going to risk using her water magic even once, not for anything.

With no warning, the wagon suddenly tilted sharply forward, and Ava was thrown off the bench and onto the floor, her stomach dropping and her dress catching on splinters.

"Going down!" she heard Gern bellow from outside.

The descent was even worse than going up had been, and Ava could only cower, her arms over her head and her knees tucked in, as the Wicked Wagon slipped out of the clouds and plummeted toward the earth.

At last there was a bone-thudding jolt, and in a rattling of wood and iron, the ride came to an end.

They were back on solid ground.

Slowly, Ava uncurled under her bench. She listened, wondering what sort of welcome she should expect from the School for Wicked Witches, but heard only silence.

The light outside the window was a flat, whitish gray. A wisp of fog oozed in between the bars.

With a clang and screech, the door flew open. To Ava's surprise, Dean Waterwash stood there, fog swirling around her like a second cloak.

"Come on," the dean snapped. "Out!"

Ava found herself reluctant to leave the wagon, but she had no choice. She stood up and stepped out.

The air smelled strange, like hot stones after the sun went down. The ground beneath her feet was crumbled black rock. The fog pressed in on all sides like ghosts. She couldn't see five feet in front of her.

"I didn't know you were coming," she said to the dean,

who was tapping an impatient foot while Gern unhitched himself from the wagon.

"Of course I came." Dean Waterwash spat every word. She looked rumpled and windswept from the flight, and very angry. "I had to make sure you and your wickedness were safely locked away!"

Gern dropped the last pole of the wagon and rolled his shoulders with a happy sigh. "All done, then?" he asked. "Last wicked wee 'un safely delivered?"

"Yes," barked Dean Waterwash. "Clearly."

"Right." The gargoyle clapped his hands. "Then I'm off. Time for me 'olidays at last! Best o' luck to ye both!" He threw Ava a grin and a wink, laughed, and took to the air with a happy clattering of his great stone wings.

Ava shivered, then looked around to find Dean Waterwash stomping away into the fog. She hurried to keep up.

Ten paces on, the dean stopped at a gnarled chunk of rock. A rusting metal pole stuck out of it, supporting a horrible-looking bell, green and dented and hanging crooked. Ava thought it looked like it had a stomachache, if that could happen to bells. Dean Waterwash seized a small mallet beside it and gave the bell five furious whacks.

The sound *hurt*. Ava yelped and winced as the echoes clanged through her head.

When she opened her eyes again, she gasped.

The fog was rolling back.

Walls of crushed stone and tangled metal soared above them, supporting a slumped, ruined collection of towers, stairs, and battlements. Windows studded with spikes gaped like broken teeth. And a gate, a cruel, twisted gate, stood open wide, waiting, leading into darkness.

The gate of the School for Wicked Witches.

Her new home.

5
THE SCHOOL FOR WICKED WITCHES

Dean Waterwash grabbed Ava by the elbow and pulled her up to the entrance.

"Here!" she shouted into the darkness. "Here's your wicked witch of the West!" She released Ava with a huff. "Well, that's done. And now I've got to exhaust myself flying back. Let's see, should I become an osprey or an albatross . . ." She glanced down at Ava. "What are you waiting for? Go in!"

Ava was shaking, though she was trying her best to hide it. She hated the feeling of the walls looming over her, and there was a bitter, acrid smell coming from the darkness.

"Couldn't I have another chance?" she pleaded. "I promise I'll be more careful! My magic just—"

"Nope! None of that!" Dean Waterwash prodded Ava in the back. "In. In!"

Ava had no choice. Scrunching up her toes, she took a step forward . . . and bonked her nose on an invisible wall blocking her path.

"Ouch!" She pressed her hands to the barrier. "What

is— Oh! Maybe the school knows I'm not supposed to be here."

"Nonsense! Look." Dean Waterwash strode forward and, to Ava's astonishment, walked past her with no problem. "Come on, girl!"

Ava tried again, but the barrier was still there.

"Hmmph." The dean tilted her head in the gloom. Then, "Oh! How irritating. I should have realized." Grumbling, she reached out, took Ava's hand, and pulled.

Ava felt a horrible, spidery tingle over every inch of her body, then she was through.

With an earsplitting groan, the gate slammed shut behind them.

They were trapped in total darkness.

Dean Waterwash snapped her fingers, and a ball of cold blue light appeared, pushing back the shadows. Blinking, Ava gazed around.

They were in a hallway of cracked greenish stone. The ceiling had tumbled down in places, leaving dark gaps above and broken shards littering the floor. The bitter smell was stronger here. It reminded Ava of an iron pot she'd once accidentally left to scorch on the fire.

"Welcome to your new school," said Dean Waterwash, striding forward. "I hope you like the look of it."

Ava did not like the look of it and was once again

working hard not to cry. Strangely, Dean Waterwash's rudeness was helping. As overwhelmed and scared as Ava felt, she would absolutely never let herself cry in front of someone so mean.

The hallway seemed like it might go on forever, but it was only a minute or two later when a red glow appeared ahead.

The glow grew brighter, and Dean Waterwash extinguished her blue orb. Together, she and Ava stepped out into a broad, circular hall.

It was as different from the great hall at West Oz Witch Academy as Ava could imagine. Sheer walls of grimy black rock rose up and up over their heads, making it feel like the bottom of an enormous well. Tilting her head back, Ava could just make out the light of sunset through an opening far above. More cracked and tumbled rock littered the floor, and dark doorways yawned from every side.

The red glow was coming from a bed of coals in the center of the room. That explained the acrid smell, too, which had gotten so strong Ava could taste it, though there was, strangely, no heat. The hall was crusted with giant bloodred crystals, some larger than Ava, skewering the floor and walls like knives. They spun the glow back and forth into a fiery shimmer, making the hall look like the inside of an oven, which made the strange cold all the more sinister.

The absolute scariest thing in the whole hall, though, was the people.

Once, when she was little, Ava had heard a story from a traveling tooth doctor about a land where hungry ghosts patrolled the streets at night, hoping to catch children out of bed. If they caught you, they drained all the warmth from your body, freezing you right there in your pajamas and carrying you off to their ghostly realm. The story had kept her from sleeping for three whole days, certain she would be taken if she closed her eyes for even a second. Now it felt as though her nightmare had come true.

Four shadowy figures floated above the bed of coals. They were wrapped in black cloaks. They were perfectly still. The figure on the left was taller than anyone Ava had ever seen.

As Ava stared, the tall figure broke its stillness and stepped lightly to the ground, coming toward them with long, hungry strides.

Dean Waterwash walked forward to meet it, and Ava scrambled after her, trying to keep close. They stopped halfway across the chamber. The figure lowered its hood.

It was a man. He had a stern, bony face, gray skin, and

black hair. His eyes glowed solid white. Cold radiated off him in waves.

"Dean Waterwash," the man said. His voice was deep and strangely echoing, as if there were more than one of him speaking.

The dean gave a nod. "Warden Pike."

"Your student is late. But I will forgive that for the pleasure of seeing the dean of West Oz Witch Academy entering my school." Warden Pike's mouth twitched. "You must be so terribly disappointed."

"It certainly hasn't been my favorite day," snapped Dean Waterwash.

"Well, at least now you will be remembered. This earns you a place in the history books alongside Dean . . . Bouncyboots, was it?"

"Dean Prancypants."

"Of course."

Ava got the distinct impression Warden Pike was enjoying himself.

"Can we get this over with?" Dean Waterwash said. "I've got a long flight home. Oh, and was that gate barrier really necessary?"

Warden Pike smiled, though it didn't reach his eyes. "I could not resist ensuring you came inside. My teachers did so want to witness this historic occasion." He gestured to the three figures still floating behind him. They lowered their hoods.

Ava swallowed a scream.

The figures had no faces. Instead, the skulls of giant birds leered out at her, their cruel beaks clicking and clacking in a kind of horrible laughter.

"Charmed," the dean muttered.

Ava's heart was galloping in her chest. Those were the teachers?! How could any of this be happening?

"Please, Dean," she burst out, grabbing at the nearest quicksilver sleeve, unable to keep her feelings in. "Please, this isn't right. I don't belong here! Just let me explain—"

"Silence!"

The word boomed through the room, and with a shock Ava realized the dean and Warden Pike had shouted it together.

"You will not embarrass me further, Ava Heartstraw," Dean Waterwash said, tugging her sleeve out of Ava's hands.

Warden Pike's eyes pierced her. "And you will obey my first rule for all students." He leaned down until his face was an inch from Ava's, the cold burning her skin. "No. Talking."

Ava could hardly imagine a worse first rule. She had to bite her tongue to keep from asking how many more there were.

She was just thinking things couldn't possibly get worse when with no warning a swarm of spiders the size of desert foxes came scurrying out of the cracks in the walls. They were a sickly yellow splotched with green, and they shimmered evilly in the red light as they formed a twitching, clicking circle around Ava and the grown-ups.

Normally, Ava liked spiders, but absolutely nothing about this place was normal, and right then she thought her skin might crawl off and run away all on its own.

Dean Waterwash regarded the new arrivals with one eyebrow raised, then turned to Ava. "Well," she said. "That's that. You'll be taken care of here, girl. And your family will be informed where you are. I believe you can send them letters once a year, though don't get your hopes up about hearing back. I'm told most families cut off contact once they're informed how wicked their child is."

Ava barely managed to stop herself from breaking the first rule again. This was horrible! Unfair! Cruel!

"As for me," Dean Waterwash said, "I hope I never see you or this place again, Warden Pike."

"It has been a great pleasure." Warden Pike gave a mocking bow. "We will speak of your visit for centuries to come. And might I suggest you depart through the roof? The gate will not open again until next year's newcomers arrive."

"Fine. Goodbye, then!"

The dean turned away, and Ava had to fight the urge to grab her sleeve again. She didn't like Dean Waterwash one bit, but the woman was her last link to West Oz, to the outside world, to everything she'd ever known before this strange, awful day. She didn't even realize she'd taken two steps after her until she heard Warden Pike growl. It took everything she had to stay put. Tears prickled behind her eyes, and her throat felt like it was stuffed with rocks.

Muttering a spell under her breath, Dean Waterwash disappeared in a flash of light, becoming an enormous seabird with a ridge of blue along its back. She beat her huge wings, knocking several of the spiders off their feet as she rose, slowly at first, then up and up and up.

They all watched until the dean reached the far-off circle of twilight and, with a glad cry, vanished into the sky, leaving Ava Heartstraw alone, surrounded by terrifying teachers, a mass of giant spiders, and the sinister fortress of crumbling stone.

6

THE SWICKWIT SECRET

Ava felt as trapped as a lizard in the claws of a rock eagle. Especially since the only people she'd seen were these four terrifying grown-ups. Where were all the other students? Were they chained to desks behind one of these dark doorways? Trapped in a dungeon under the boiling lake? Or had they been fed to the spiders?

She raised her chin, clenching her hands in her burlap dress. Whatever was coming might be a nightmare, but she was going to try her best to get through it.

Warden Pike stared down at her.

"Well, Miss Heartstraw." Her name sounded strange in his echoing voice. "What do you think happens now?"

Ava tried to swallow. "Now you believe me that this is all a mistake, and send me back to WOW Academy?"

"Wrong," Warden Pike said. "Very wrong. Now we eat . . ." He pointed one long finger at her. "Dinner."

Warden Pike snapped his fingers, and everything changed.

The three floating teachers settled to the floor and transformed, their bird-skull heads and sinister cloaks melting away to reveal round old women. They might have been triplets, with their wrinkly orange skin, pointy chins, and sharp eyes, but the one on the left, dressed in green, had magnificent antlers sprouting from her head. The one in the middle, all in gray, had hands made of what looked like solid gold. And the one on the right, smoothing her copper-colored robes, had six eyes.

Ava didn't have time to stare, however, because the school itself was transforming. The heavy stones lying everywhere were flying up like thistledown, notching back into place in the broken walls. Cracks sealed, arching windows popped into existence, and the dust and grime vanished, leaving the floor and walls a glossy, shining black.

The enormous red crystals changed next, transforming into a crowd of kids in gray robes. They had to jump aside for the spiders, whose twitching legs and eyes became more kids, older this time, all dressed in copper.

The ex-spider kids were shaking out their limbs when the glowing bed of coals surged out of the floor, separating into a dozen teenagers wearing midnight black. They looked impressively confident and powerful as they joined the others, talking and laughing, one or two of them still glowing.

The cold that had filled the hall was gone, as was the

bitter smell, which had been replaced by a pleasant aroma of dried herbs and lightning. Cool evening light streamed in through the arched windows, making the space feel a little like the train station at Muzzlewump, grand and expectant and interesting.

Ava gaped around. This was . . . not what she'd been expecting.

She looked up to find Warden Pike watching her. He looked just the same, though his voice only sounded like one person as he said, "Welcome to the real School for Wicked Witches."

Ava had to open and close her mouth a few times. "Then what— What was going on before?" she asked. "With the crumbling castle and everything?"

"That is an act we keep up. As far as the outside world is concerned, this place is exactly as we presented it, since for some reason people feel safer thinking their wicked children are locked away in a terrible prison." Warden Pike quirked one corner of his mouth. "I must admit we enjoy putting on a show at the start of every year."

"So this isn't really a scary school for punishing kids?"

"That is not the truth of Swickwit, no."

"Swickwit?"

"Our name for this place. The other schools focus on

making their students as similar as possible. This is a haven for children who are different, a home where those the world has labeled misfits can explore their magic in peace. And where we can guide young people with . . . unique powers in the wisest ways to use them."

Relief shimmered through Ava like spring rain. "You mean no one here is wicked?"

"We are all capable of being wicked, Ava. Some students here very much incline that way, others less so."

Ava's relief evaporated. "But— No. I mean, *I'm* not! My magic might be bad sometimes when I'm feeling angry and stuff— I'm not really sure about that yet. But I'm definitely not wicked, and if you just let me go back to West Oz and explain, I'm sure I could—"

"Enough." Warden Pike knelt down, making his eerie white eyes level with hers. "WOW Academy has said you do not belong there, Ava. That makes you one of us. Besides, you know the secret of Swickwit now. If the other schools ever found out, they would band together and force us to become exactly what we pretend to be. We have kept this secret for almost a thousand years, and we cannot risk anyone giving it away. So, no, you cannot go back. You cannot leave at all. No student departs Swickwit until I decide they are old and wise enough to be trusted."

Ava opened her mouth to argue, but Warden Pike rose to his full towering height. "You will understand in time."

A bell clanged somewhere overhead, and the noise in the hall increased as the students and teachers began heading for one of the doorways.

"The signal for dinner," explained Warden Pike. "We are eating late thanks to you, Miss Heartstraw, so orientation will take place tomorrow. For tonight, enjoy your first meal at Swickwit." He began to walk away, then turned back, giving her a fierce, appraising look. "We are happy to have a west witch among us again," he said. "We expect astonishing things from you."

He disappeared into the chattering crowd, and amid a swirl of robes and more than a few curious glances, Ava was carried along into the depths of her unexpectedly complicated new home.

7

A NEW HOME

Ava wondered how many more stairs there could possibly be. The school was a maze of hallways, courtyards, and towers, and she was super grateful to the gray-robed girl who had finally pointed her toward the first-year dorms. She was less grateful that they seemed to be at the top of a never-ending staircase.

Dinner had been a chaotic affair. Swickwit students, it turned out, dined in an old ballroom lit by dozens of mismatched chandeliers and stuffed to its mirrored walls with armchairs and decorative tables. Ava had settled on a footstool in a corner while the rest of the students dragged the furniture around, gathering into noisy, happy groups. Their robes turned the dining hall into a sea of copper and gray, with the dozen teenagers in black sprinkled in like ravens. There had also been one tall boy in green sitting all alone like her. Seeing him had made Ava glance up at the teachers' table, wondering if there might be some connection between him and the green-robed teacher with the antlers.

She'd spotted some of her fellow first-year kids when

she got up to get food. They were easy to pick out by the different clothes they wore, and they'd separated into little groups—probably based on where they were from, Ava guessed. She'd felt too shy to ask to sit with any of them. What if they all turned out to be mean and wicked? Or worse, what if they were nice, but they all said no?

Copying the older students, she'd gotten her dinner by sliding a tray into a gap in a painting of a kitchen, then grabbing it as it shot back out, heavy with food. Luckily, most of the dishes had looked somewhat familiar. She'd eaten on her footstool, the tray balanced on her knees, watching the older kids shout and joke and tease one another with magic. The ballroom echoed with noise and clamor, and the lights and faces reflected over and over again in the mirrors, and by the time Warden Pike ordered everyone to bed she was feeling so overwhelmed she completely missed the instructions on where she was supposed to go.

Now, as she climbed, her head swirled with questions: Would every meal here be like that? What about classes? Where did the food come from? What did the robe colors mean? Would she ever make any friends?

Everything was happening so fast!

At last the stairs ended, and Ava found herself stepping up into a wide, round room settled like a bird's nest at the top of the tower she'd just climbed. The walls were stone, but the floor and ceiling were honey-colored wood. Soft, buttery light came from lamps set in niches, making the space feel surprisingly cozy and inviting. Silvery letters in the floor caught Ava's eye, and she did a circle around the stairs to read them: *N-E-T-T-L-E*. What did that mean?

Benches lined the walls of the room, with four closed doors set between them, each with a silver nameplate. Ava went to read the nearest.

CLASSROOM.

The next door read LIBRARY, then LABORATORY, and finally DORMS.

Ava's stomach squeezed as she pushed the DORMS door open. Her new classmates had to have gotten here before her. Were they already in bed? Had any of them been talking about her?

The door opened into a hallway with more doors on either side. Ava headed down it, reading silver nameplates to her left and right as she went.

BRANWEN (EAST)

JADIS FROST (NORTH)

MATTHEW AVALON (NORTH)

JONSI HULDU (NORTH)

MARGO ASPIC (EAST)

CARMELIE WRIGHT (SOUTH)

DORIAN COB (SOUTH)

WOLFGANG HEX (EAST)

BERYL KRALEXANDER (EAST)

OPAL HAVNOR (SOUTH)

The last door on the right had only one name: CROW BACKPATCH (EAST). Though someone had stuck a piece of paper underneath that said *Welcome back! Again!* in scrawly handwriting.

The last door on the left had two nameplates on it: TINABELLA GROUSE (NORTH) and AVA HEARTSTRAW (WEST).

Ava swallowed. She hoped her roommate was someone nice. And quiet. All she wanted to do right then was fall into bed and sleep.

Smoothing down her cactus dress, she turned the handle and stepped through. She had one brief glimpse of a small room with two sets of matching furniture before there was a scream, the sound of running feet, and a girl appeared out of nowhere and dumped a bucket of water over her head.

8

A ROOMMATE AND A RESOLUTION

Ava stood in the doorway, shocked, soaked, and dripping.

Her attacker was a head shorter than Ava, with silvery skin and black hair cut into a bob. She wore a fancy purple sweatsuit and was still holding the bucket, watching Ava with her chin thrust forward.

"Huh," said the girl after a moment. "That wasn't what I expected."

"Same here." Ava stepped into the room. The door closed behind her.

The girl set the bucket on the floor. "I had to try, though," she said in a brisk, confident voice. "You are the witch from West Oz, right?"

"Um, yes. And try what, exactly?"

"To find out how wicked you are!"

"And you thought throwing water on me would help?"

The girl shrugged. "It was something I read somewhere. West Oz wicked witches are supposed to be extra bad, and I have *zero* interest in putting up with a super-wicked roommate. So when I saw your name on the door,

I decided to see if I could just get rid of you and have the room to myself. I'm not wicked at all, you see. I was framed."

Ava forgot about being wet. She almost melted with relief. "Oh!" she said. "Same! I mean, I wasn't framed, but I don't think I'm wicked, either!"

The girl's eyes went extra wide. "Truly? Don't mess with me. I always get revenge on people who mess with me."

"Truly!" said Ava. "I'm good. It was all a mistake. My magic just kind of got out of control." Her stomach gave a swoop as she said it. She wasn't exactly lying, but she also wasn't sharing the full truth. It was definitely a good thing that this girl hadn't seen what actually happened in the WOW Academy great hall.

The girl eyed her for a considering moment, then thrust out a hand. "We'd better be friends, then. Tinabella Grouse."

"Ava Heartstraw."

"Ew, your hand's wet."

"I think that's because you threw a bucket of water on me?"

"Oh, yeah. Well, there's towels and stuff in your closet. That's yours there, along with your dresser and bed. Bathroom's through that door." She threw the whole room a sour look. "This place is such a dump. Guess it could always be worse, though."

Ava blinked. She thought their room looked amazing. She'd never slept in a bed before, let alone had her own closet or dresser. Back home she had a shelf under the sink that was hers, but it was mostly taken up with tortoise supplies for Peaches. With twelve kids and almost no money, everything else in the Heartstraw household had to be shared.

Tinabella already had a mess of books lying open on her bed, and she flopped down in the middle of them while Ava explored.

Her closet contained seven uniforms in exactly her size—pants, shirts, sweaters, and robes—while the dresser held towels and three sets of pajamas. And all of it was green. The exact same green, she noticed, that the boy sitting alone in the dining hall had been wearing. The same green as the teacher with the antlers. Ava wondered what it all meant.

The tiny, tidy bathroom smelled like rosemary and peppermint. Ava dried off and changed into the green pajamas, which were soft and cozy, then hung her burlap dress neatly on her closet door.

She looked around, feeling homesickness squeeze her ribs. Apart from the dress with its embroidered cactuses nothing here was familiar. It was all strange and new. She tried to picture this room becoming her home over days, months, even years, but couldn't.

Still, so far Swickwit wasn't nearly as bad as she'd expected. Maybe nothing here would be? Then she remembered what Warden Pike had said about everyone here being a little wicked—some less so, but some definitely more.

"What are the other new kids like?" she asked Tinabella.

Her roommate waved a hand, her eyes glued to the page she was reading. "Fine. Wicked, mostly, at least the ones from North Oz. I hardly remember."

Ava thought she would have remembered plenty about anyone she'd flown in the Wicked Wagon with, but she tried another question as she settled cross-legged on her bed.

"What's it like in the North?"

Tinabella looked up, her dark eyes shining. "Oh, it is just *perfect*! My whole family is magical, and we're so rich. We've got five houses and eight swimming pools and nineteen horses, and there are juicy-pop trees literally everywhere . . ."

Her words came pouring out, describing a world Ava had never even imagined. As an only child, Tinabella had received everything she ever wanted, from her own full-size library to a toothbrush decorated with rainbow-colored diamonds. Her life had been going perfectly until her magic test at North Oz Witch Academy, when somehow her demonstration went wrong and she got stamped as wicked. Tinabella was certain she knew what had really happened, though. Timmybob Pheasant, the only son of her family's archrivals, had been in line right behind her, and he must have sabotaged her somehow.

"So obviously I cannot wait to get back there, like, immediately and get my revenge," she finished.

Ava sat up as straight as a desert cricket. "Wait, you're going back? How?"

Tinabella shrugged. "I'll figure something out. I *refuse* to let Timmybob win. I'm going back to North Oz Witch Academy if it's the last thing I do. I mean, it's literally the school's motto: *Not North Oz? Say No Way*. So that's what I'm doing."

"West Oz's motto is *When people meet a West Oz witch, they say WOW*," said Ava.

"Seriously?"

"Pretty sure."

"That's weird."

It was Ava's turn to shrug.

"I wonder if Swickwit has a motto." Tinabella shuffled her books. "Hmm, probably not in any of these. I'll raid the library again tomorrow." She stopped and looked up. "What am I saying? I don't care about this place! I only care about getting out!"

"Same!" said Ava. "Do you think we should try talking to Warden Pike? He told me no one ever leaves until they're wise or whatever, but maybe together we can get him to really listen, and—"

"Nope," interrupted Tinabella. "Not a chance. You missed this whole speech he gave before. We know the big Swickwit secret now, so they won't let us out until we're old. Like, *twenty*. Believe me." She waved at her books. "I've been researching ever since dinner. The only way we're getting out is if we escape."

Escape. The word sent a happy shiver down Ava's back. She really shouldn't be here, after all, and she didn't want to go nine whole years without seeing her family just because a bunch of grown-ups had made a mistake about her. It wasn't right. It wasn't fair.

But *how* would they escape? Everything she'd heard made it sound impossible.

Tinabella, disappearing into the bathroom with her own pajamas, already had ideas.

"We'll need to get our bearings first," she yelled from behind the door. "Learn the geography of the school, probe for weak spots, that sort of thing. We've got to be organized."

"Okay," said Ava. "Do you think—"

"Then once we find an opening, we can sneak out. At night, probably."

"That's a good—"

"But the most important thing is not to trust *anyone*. It's got to be just you and me, or someone will discover what we're doing and then the teachers could lock us up in the dungeons or something."

Ava waited.

The bathroom door opened. "Well? Don't you agree?" Tinabella thrust her chin out above her green pajamas.

"Yup," said Ava. "Sounds good. I agree."

"Excellent!" Tinabella swept the books from her bed onto the floor and flopped back against her pillow. "It's a plan. Tomorrow, we learn our way around this place from top to bottom. Then we figure out how to sneak out of it." She waved a hand at Ava. "Get the lamps, will you?"

Ava turned off the lights and climbed into bed. It was super comfortable, and she couldn't believe she got an entire blanket all to herself and her very own pillow. She stretched out as far as she could, curling her toes.

With the room dark, the window let in a faint glow from the constant fog outside. "At least the view's familiar," Tinabella said with a yawn. "It's always foggy in North Oz."

"We never get it in the desert," said Ava. "Sometimes there's a haze, but that burns off pretty quick once the sun climbs over the dunes . . ." She trailed off, thinking of the smell of the sand in the morning. Her brothers and sisters making food, going over the day's chore list. Her parents already heading out to check the bricks. The long hard day starting out cool and beautiful. The ravens croaking in the cactus tree.

A lonely ache flooded her insides.

But she had to be strong.

Ava rolled over, facing the dark and her very first night away from home, deciding to focus on only good things.

She had a friend now. They were coming up with a plan. She would be back where she belonged very, very soon.

9

FIRST BREAKFAST

Ava woke to the sound of screaming.

"What—what's going on?" she mumbled, struggling upright. "What's happening?"

Blinking, she saw morning light streaming through the window. The roofs and towers of the school floated amid the shifting fog rising from the boiling lake. The sun sparkled with rainbows over the hills of broken glass. Taken together, it would have been a beautiful view to start the day—if it wasn't all keeping Ava trapped somewhere she didn't want to be.

The screaming was still echoing down the hall.

Already on her feet and looking grumpy, Tinabella yanked open the door and marched out. "Hey!" she yelled. "What's the big idea? Some of us are trying to sleep!"

There was more yelling, and a moment later she was back.

"Breakfast," she said, rolling her eyes. "A fight over the waffles. We might as well join in now we're up."

"What are waffles?" Ava asked.

Tinabella's jaw hit the floor. "Get dressed," she said. "Now."

Five minutes later, Ava was halfway through her first-ever waffle, and she thought she understood what all the screaming had been about.

The round room had transformed into a sort of mini dining hall. The stairs were gone somehow, and a table filled the center of the space, stacked with plates and food and napkins. Some of the food was familiar to Ava—oatmeal, toast, and one or two of the fruits—but plenty of other things, like the waffles and a steaming mound of crispy green meat, were a total mystery. She was grateful Tinabella was there to guide her.

They ate on one of the benches along the wall, watching the other kids, who had all paired off or formed clumps. There was only one boy sitting by himself, and Ava realized it was the tall boy in green she'd noticed in the dining hall. He was wearing the same robes, and this close up she realized he was at least a couple of years older than the rest of them. She wondered what his story was, and what he was doing among the first-year students.

Tinabella was stealing the very last bite of waffle off Ava's plate when a strikingly good-looking boy and girl peeled away from the biggest clump of kids and headed their way. The pair stopped in front of them, crossed their arms in unison, and stared down at Ava.

"I bet I'm wickeder than you," announced the girl, without even saying hello. She had pale pink skin and hair a hundred different shades of sunset orange, and she was smiling much too wide. Ava was instantly reminded of Sheridan back at WOW Academy.

She swallowed her mouthful of toast. "Huh?"

"You heard me." The girl tossed her head, making her hair swirl beautifully around her. "I'm Carmelie Wright. This is Dorian Cob. He's really wicked, too. But not as wicked as me. No one's as wicked as me. Not even some show-off from West Oz."

The boy beside her nodded. He had golden skin, dark wavy hair, and dimples.

"In fact," continued the girl, "I bet you're not even average. I bet you're the least wicked witch here."

"Well, yeah," said Ava. "That's right. At least I hope so."

Carmelie had obviously been expecting a different reaction. She frowned in confusion. Tinabella gave Ava a nudge.

"Oh, except for Tinabella," Ava added. "She and I are tied."

Tinabella tsked. "I didn't mean that! I meant stop

talking to her. We're avoiding all the wicked kids, remember?"

"Yes! Right. Sorry." Ava looked down, meaning to carry on eating, but found her plate was empty. She tapped it awkwardly with her fork.

"Sooo, wait," said Carmelie. "Do you two think you're actually good or something? Like, you got sent here by mistake?" Her face lit up with glee. "That is too, *too* funny!"

Ava bit her tongue to keep from replying, but this time Tinabella answered.

"Funny?" she said, her voice low and threatening. "Did you just call me *funny*?" She dropped her plate on the bench and got to her feet, which would have been more impressive if she weren't a foot shorter than Carmelie.

"I may not be wicked," she growled, "but I can still make your life miserable. I could turn your hands into honey and your face into a fish and your shadow into a hungry bear if I wanted, you . . . you . . . pine-headed moss masher!"

Carmelie stared down at Tinabella, her eyes wide, and Ava braced herself for what might happen next.

To her surprise, a corner of Carmelie's mouth curled into a smile.

"I like you," she said, pointing at Tinabella. "You've

got fire. Let me know when you're done playing goodie-two-slippers with this loser, and we can hang out."

"What did you just call my roommate?!" Tinabella demanded. She was practically standing on Carmelie's toes now, her head tilted back so she could glare into her face. Ava was surprised smoke wasn't coming out of her ears. For the first time, she wondered what Tinabella's magic actually was. She was pretty certain it couldn't be any of those scary things she'd been threatening.

Pretty certain.

All the other kids around the room were watching the Tinabella-Carmelie face-off. Ava felt a wave of relief that she wasn't the one making a scene this time, then an immediate twist of guilt. Did thinking that make her bad? Was she actually becoming wicked? Had letting her magic run wild even just once started her down a slippery slope?

At that moment the door marked CLASSROOM flew open, slamming into the wall with a bang that made everyone jump and look around.

Ava forgot her worries and swallowed in fear.

The CLASSROOM door led into complete and total darkness.

"Enter!" boomed a voice from somewhere inside. "Class is now in session!"

10

FIRST CLASS

To Ava's surprise the tall boy moved first, walking calmly across the room and straight into the darkness like he'd done it a hundred times before.

One by one, exchanging nervous glances, the rest of them followed.

Ava entered the darkness and immediately felt herself go completely weightless.

The world lost all direction. A cold like she'd never imagined burned down to her bones. A yawning sense of endless horror flashed across her mind.

Then she was through, and light and warmth returned as she stepped into a classroom.

It was a strange space, somewhere between creepy and cozy. The floor was dark slate, and there were comfy desks in rows facing a movable blackboard with a window behind it. But the curving walls and ceiling were made entirely of gnarled, twisted roots writhing slowly over and around each other. They were clearly alive, though Ava couldn't tell how, and the faint, dry rasping they made as they moved gave her the shivers.

Standing in front of the blackboard was the green-clad teacher with the antlers. She was shorter than Ava remembered, barely as tall as most of the students, but her antlers seemed to have grown by at least a foot. There were tiny charms tied to them, twinkling in the light streaming through the window.

"Sit, sit!" the teacher called. She had a deep, powerful voice, and was obviously used to using it. "Quickly now, anywhere. Right, all here? Thirteen students? Yes. So, welcome! You're wondering about the darkness on the way in? That was just a little housekeeping. A quick trip through the void to clean off any curses or spirit leeches or similar nasties. We don't *mind* them, of course, but they do tend to interfere with learning. And it looks like some of you were dripping with them! I counted four curses, five brain gnats, and one very bad case of Exploding Knees that was about to cause someone a great deal of excitement. Oh, stop looking so horrified; we only need to do it once. All gone now! All lost in the void. Today you start fresh."

Ava was already having trouble keeping up. Beside her, Tinabella was leaning forward, squinting in concentration.

"Right!" the teacher charged on. "Here's what we're doing." She rapped her knuckles on the blackboard, and a list appeared in scrawly handwriting. "Step one: I'm going to introduce myself. Step two: I'll give you the rundown on how Swickwit works. Step three: We'll go over class rules. Step four: You'll introduce yourselves and demonstrate your wicked magic for the class. We need to get all of that done before break in ninety minutes, then we'll talk spells until lunch. Any questions?"

She did not wait for questions.

"Excellent! My name is Professor Mulch, I have been teaching here at Swickwit for ninety-seven years, and now would be an appropriate time to applaud."

She waited. There were five seconds of awkward silence while the class caught up, then everyone clapped.

"Thank you, thank you." Professor Mulch bowed, her antlers almost scraping the desks in the front row. "So! I teach Nettle, which means you. Nettle is the first level of study here at Swickwit. We do not have grades based on age here. What sense is that? Instead, we have four levels of witchcraft based on *skill*: Nettle, Cobweb, Cauldron, and Broom. Open your spell books, please!"

Spell books? Ava glanced at Tinabella. Tinabella glanced at Ava. Everyone else looked just as confused except over in the corner, where the tall boy somehow had a thick book open on his desk, along with a silver pencil.

Carmelie Wright raised her hand.

"Speak!" barked Professor Mulch.

"I'm sorry, Professor," Carmelie said in a syrupy-sweet voice. "But we don't seem to have any books yet."

"What?!" Professor Mulch pressed her hands over her eyes, took a deep breath, and let out a piercing shriek. A rain of books fell down, slamming squarely onto each desk.

Ava put a hand to her racing heart. Three minutes into her first class and she felt like she'd been digging sand pits all day without a break.

The book in front of her was thick and heavy and wrapped in sky-blue leather. It was also blank inside.

"What's going on?" hissed Tinabella, flipping through her own blank book, which was a rusty blood red.

"What's going on," hollered Professor Mulch, "is you've just received your first spell books! They're blank because you have to fill them in by learning. And don't bother whispering in here, little nettles, these catch everything." She pointed up at her antlers. "Right, you'll need pencils for taking notes, if you want them."

She snapped her fingers, making a silver pencil pop into existence on each desk. Another snap, and every spell book in the classroom opened itself to page one. Ava watched as words filled the page, spelling out everything Professor Mulch had told them about herself so far.

"All right, we're up to step two." Professor Mulch slapped the blackboard, and Ava's book turned the page. More words appeared, this time with orderly headings. "Who wants to read first? You! Yes, you. Nice and loud now."

A girl up front gave an awkward cough and started reading from her book.

Ava read along.

LEVEL 1: NETTLE

Focus: First-year basics. Raising magical force. Appearances. Protection. Staying focused. Simple light magic. Getting a handle on your wickedness. Juggling.

Color: Green

Teacher: Coleus Mulch

Term: One year, followed by testing to advance to Cobweb.

"New reader!"

Everyone jumped. Professor Mulch stabbed a finger at another girl, who read the next section in a quavering voice.

LEVEL 2: COBWEB
Focus: Advanced theory. Elemental magic. Summoning. Weather. Illusion. Making wickedness work for you. Improv.
Color: Gray
Teacher: Parlous Nightshade
Term: Undefined. Average three years. Monthly testing opportunity.

"You!"

A boy behind Ava read next.

LEVEL 3: CAULDRON
Focus: Specialization. Independent study. Teaching seminars. The art of hiding wickedness. Pickleball.
Color: Copper
Teacher: Contumacious Dust
Term: Undefined. Average four years.

"Final reader!"

Ava's insides somersaulted as she looked up to find Professor Mulch pointing at her. Luckily, the last section was short. And surprising . . .

LEVEL 4: BROOM

Focus: Mind your own business.
Color: Black
Teacher: Warden Threnody Pike
Term: Until finished.

There was an outbreak of murmuring. Ava understood why. She had questions, too.

"Clear enough?" said Professor Mulch. "I get you set up with all the basics in Nettle, then at the end of the year you test into Cobweb and start the really fun stuff."

The girl who'd read first raised her hand.

"If Nettle only lasts one year, how come *he* was already wearing green last night?" She gestured with a thumb at the tall boy. "And how come he's so much older than us?"

The boy, who had been doodling in his spell book, glanced up as everyone turned to look at him. He gave a shy little wave.

"Ah, Crow Backpatch, our determined trier." Professor Mulch's smile was genuinely kind this time. "Say hello to your new classmates, Crow."

"Hello." Crow had a deep, scratchy voice, just like the bird he was named after.

"This will be Crow's third try at Nettle—a new Swickwit record." Professor Mulch sounded fond and exasperated at the same time. "He's got plenty of power locked away somewhere; we just haven't found a way to get his brain—if he has one—in control of it yet. But maybe this is our year? We all hope so!"

Carmelie and the girl beside her put their heads together, whispering and giggling, and most of the other students openly smirked. Ava felt bad for Crow. He seemed sweet.

Dorian Cob, who'd been frowning down at his spell book, raised a hand. "Hey, how do you get into Broom, Professor? There's nothing in here about testing at the end of Cauldron."

Professor Mulch's mouth split into a very different smile, a wide, wet grin, revealing more than the usual number of teeth. She wagged a finger. "Ah-ah-ah. Only teachers and Broom students are allowed to know that, little mealworm. Get into Broom in eight or so years, and you'll find out absolutely everything. And probably wish you hadn't!"

She cackled, and Ava felt a cold shiver down her spine.

"Time for step three!" Professor Mulch yelled. She slapped the blackboard, and once again their spell books filled in on their own. This time, though, Professor Mulch led them through the contents.

"All right: Class rules and things to know! You are

currently in Nettle Tower. The round room you ate breakfast in is your common area and is called, creatively, the Round Room. You will wear your green Nettle uniforms every single day. Raise your hand to talk in class. Side chat and whisper among yourselves all you want, but remember that I can hear every word and will repeat what you say to the class if I feel like it. You are allowed to be late to class *once* across the entire year. The second time, I will turn you into a desk for twenty-four hours and you will spend all of it here in the classroom practicing being early.

"As you will have noticed, there are currently no stairs in or out of Nettle Tower, and the library and laboratory doors are locked. That is because morning classes are absolutely mandatory, so there's no need for other places to be. Your afternoons, however, are your own. Every day after lunch the doors will unlock, the stairs will be back, and you will be free to explore the school, do your own research and learning, or waste time running around causing trouble until dinner."

There was a buzz of excited murmuring at this news. Tinabella punched Ava on the arm, and their eyes met. Free afternoons! That was perfect for their plans.

"You will be held fully responsible for any actions you take during your free time." Professor Mulch gave them all a very pointed look that set the charms in her antlers swinging, then continued. "The laboratory door takes you to a fully equipped magic laboratory on the other side of the school; use it however you like but please do not blow yourselves up. The library door transports you to the main Swickwit library. Yes, they are both portals, and no, we will not be teaching you portal magic. Please do not attempt to learn portal magic if you value keeping all your internal organs on the inside."

A boy in front of Ava turned green and put a hand over his mouth.

"Things to know while exploring Swickwit!" Professor Mulch bellowed. "There are plenty of places in the school you will not be able to go. Some because you do not have the magical skill yet, some because you do not know the passwords, some because they are infested with spiny scab fleas and you are sensible enough not to want to have your veins filled with stinging insects. By all means go ahead and try getting into places you're not supposed to be! Just be willing to face the wide variety of possible consequences.

"Most important of all, you should know that so long as you are in the green uniform of Nettle, none of the other students here will speak to or acknowledge you."

This got another round of murmuring from the class.

"Students in gray, copper, or black will talk to each other, but not to you. They will not get out of your way, make room for you at dinner, or pull you out of a haunted well. This is one of Swickwit's oldest and strictest customs, so remember: The people in this room are all you've got until you get into Cobweb."

Heads turned as the Nettle students looked at one another, taking in the news.

Ava's own head was feeling as stuffed as a cactus after a flash flood. She gave her spell book a pat, grateful everything was written down. She'd hate to forget any of this and accidentally get in trouble.

Then she remembered she wasn't planning on staying.

"That's it for step three!" Professor Mulch roared. "Now it's my turn to learn about *you* as we uncover the wicked magic that brought you all here in the first place."

11

CLASSMATES

"Just step four left, little nettles!" Professor Mulch bellowed. "And then we all get a break. We'll go alphabetically by last name. When I call you, come up front, tell us where you're from, and demonstrate the magic that got you sent to Swickwit. Anyone want to guess why we're doing this?"

She did not wait for guesses.

"Because the magic you can already do is your key to learning the rest, correct. I want to see exactly where each of you is starting from, so no tricks! No showing off! And no funny business!" She pulled a sheet of paper out of thin air and studied it. "Right. Branwen?"

A girl in the front row raised her hand.

"Since you don't seem to have a last name, you'd better go first." Professor Mulch yanked one of the charms from her antlers and hurled it against the wall, where it transformed into a squashy armchair. Settling into it, she shouted for the sharing to begin.

The girl with no last name rose and stood beside the blackboard. She had paper-white skin, a razor-sharp jaw, and the longest, pointiest fingers Ava had ever seen.

"Hi, I'm Branwen," she said, in a surprisingly sweet voice. "I'm from East Oz. And I got sent here because I can do this." She twirled a hand, and all the shadows in the room lifted free from the floor and corners. They clotted together into one dark, ominous mass, stretching out over the other students, looming like a wall of night at the end of the world. Ava heard several frightened gasps. Then, with another twirl of Branwen's fingers, the shadows zipped back to their places like nothing had happened. Branwen returned to her desk, and everyone blinked and looked around, clearly impressed.

Margo Aspic, also from East Oz, was next. She had coppery skin, wore her brown hair in a sort of sand dune on top of her head, and spoke very formally. "When I perform a song," she told them, "people get stuck. I shall demonstrate."

She sang the opening lines of a popular tune about chickens, and with the very first notes Ava felt her entire body lock in place. She could still breathe and blink, and her heart kept beating, but she couldn't so much as twitch a fingertip. Margo walked around the classroom, adjusting spell books, moving pencils, tapping people on the head, and smiling a very worrying smile as she sang.

Ava sighed with relief when Margo finally stopped and sat back down. It was a horrible feeling being trapped. Also, Margo was not a very good singer.

"Matthew Avalon?" called Professor Mulch. "You're up!"

Matthew Avalon was a worried-looking boy with lavender skin and no hair or eyebrows. "Um, I'm from North Oz," he said. "And I need a volunteer?"

A white-haired girl in the front punched a fist in the air. Matthew went over to her desk. "I, uh, need to touch your hand, please?" The girl offered her palm. Matthew placed a finger on it, shuddered, and closed his eyes.

"Okay," he said. "When you were six, your older brother stole your favorite umbrella. You chased him into the woods trying to get it back, and he fell down a ravine and broke his arm and you got in huge trouble. He still shows you the scar when he wants something, and—"

The girl snatched her hand away, her honey-colored face darkening. "So, what?" she demanded. "When you touch people, you see the worst memory of their life, or something?"

"The worst memory of their life *so far*," Matthew said apologetically.

Everyone edged away from him as he returned to his seat.

"Crow?" Professor Mulch called. "Want to give this another shot?"

Ava leaned forward along with the rest of the class as the tall kid got up. What was his deal? Why did he have to keep repeating Nettle?

"Hello," the boy said, once he'd reached the front. "I'm Crow Backpatch. I'm from East Oz. And I can only do one thing with magic."

He stood there. Seconds ticked by.

Nothing happened.

The students began shooting one another glances.

"Is he doing it?" Tinabella muttered.

Crow scratched his neck.

Over in her armchair, Professor Mulch was looking disappointed.

"Still nothing, Crow?" she called.

Crow shrugged. "It's still too dangerous."

Professor Mulch waved him back to his seat.

Handsome Dorian Cob jumped up next, swaggering to the front. Ava rolled her eyes. Whatever Dorian's magic was, she was already not impressed.

"My name is Dorian." He gave them all a wide smile, flashing his dimples. "I come from beautiful South Oz, and I can do this."

Dorian tapped a finger to his forehead, then pointed it

at Matthew Avalon. There was a soft crinkling sound, and the next moment Matthew's face had become a perfect copy of Dorian's.

Most of the class gasped. Matthew, looking horrified, felt his new face. Carmelie laughed and applauded. Dorian wore a huge, wolfish grin as he began changing all their faces rapid-fire one after another, filling the classroom with his golden skin and dark wavy hair. Everyone was talking now, staring around at the same face on so many bodies. Dorian was just about to reach Ava when—

"Cob!" Professor Mulch's bellow cut through the excitement. "What did I say about showing off?"

The wild look in Dorian's eyes faded under the professor's glare. "Um, don't?"

"So why are you? Change everyone back and sit down."

His cheeks flushing dusky pink, Dorian did as he was told.

Jadis Frost from North Oz went after Dorian. She had the same silvery skin as Tinabella, though with patches of blue, and her magic was to turn stone so cold it shattered. It only worked on stone, apparently, which Ava thought was a very good thing after watching Jadis gleefully dismember a statue Professor Mulch conjured for her.

Tinabella was next. Ava felt a nervous shiver watching her roommate stomp to the front. Tinabella had said she wasn't wicked, but what if her power actually was something scary?

She shouldn't have worried, though, since Tinabella turned out to have the power to become invisible—although only while she was running.

"It's not super useful," panted an invisible Tinabella, running in place. "Since you can always hear my feet."

Ava clapped silently as Tinabella sat back down beside her, wondering how exactly invisible running could have made the North Oz Witch Academy think her roommate was wicked. She thought it looked fun.

It was Opal Havnor from South Oz's turn next. She had dark brown skin and a crown of beautiful bronze hair. When she wiggled her ears, everyone's fingernails grew and grew until they were dragging on the floor, then wrapped around their desks and chairs like ropes. The whole class was very relieved when Opal stopped wiggling her ears and their nails shrank back to normal.

"Ava Heartstraw," shouted Professor Mulch.

There was a rustling as the whole class sat up, every eye following Ava as she made her way to the front. It looked like all her classmates were excited to see what spectacular magic had made her the first wicked witch of the West in two hundred years.

Ava hoped she was going to disappoint them.

Back in the Wicked Wagon, she'd promised herself she wouldn't risk using her water powers again, not even once. But it would be kind of a shame not to learn anything while she was here, and Professor Mulch had just said their first magic was the key to all the rest.

Could she chance using a teeny bit of power? She wasn't angry at Sheridan this time, and she wouldn't try to show off like Dorian. And if there was even a hint of her losing control, she would do her best to stop.

Her palms began to sweat as she looked out across the small classroom. If this went wrong, if her powers really were wicked and she did anything like what she'd done back at WOW Academy, people could really get hurt.

Her conscience prickled, but it was too late to back out now.

She decided to start with something familiar.

"Can I have a cactus, please?" she asked.

Muttering broke out as Professor Mulch magicked up a cactus in a little pot. Swallowing down her fear, Ava reached for her power.

Water bloomed in her mind, and for one terrible moment she thought she'd lost control already. Then she sucked in a breath, and the tension eased. The air here had plenty of water in it, true, but there were no plants growing in Nettle Tower—she couldn't sense a single thing from the root ceiling and walls—and none of her classmates were holding hot chocolate or juicy red apples this time. Most of what she could sense came from outside, where the fog and the boiling lake thrummed with a power she was doing her absolute best to ignore.

Another breath, and Ava narrowed her focus down to the smallest wisp of water she could, then began feeding it into the cactus.

It wasn't exactly like working with brick moss, but it was close. She could feel the roots growing under the soil, and everyone in the classroom could see the little white flowers unfurling up the cactus's sides between the spikes. So far, things were going well.

Pleased, Ava tried using a bit more water, and the cactus shot up several inches before she caught herself. She looked around, worried, but the rest of the class were all doodling in their spell books or staring out the window. Even Tinabella was looking bored and disappointed.

Professor Mulch, on the other hand, was eyeing her intently.

"Is that all you have to show us?" she called. "You're sure that's the most you can do?"

Ava nodded, and after another long stare the professor waved her back to her seat. On the way, she heard Carmelie whisper, "So, what, she makes boring plants grow a little bit? What kind of wicked talent is that?"

Ava dropped into her desk feeling incredibly relieved. She had done it! Her magic hadn't gone wicked, and she'd kept control almost the entire time. Hopefully this meant she could start learning other, safer kinds of magic now. Hopefully this was a breakthrough that would stick.

The next student to present was a short, round boy from East Oz named Wolfgang Hex. He had olive skin, a pillar of spiky gray hair, and a nasal voice. When he held his breath, sparks popped into life all around him. The longer he held his breath the more sparks there were, until Wolfgang disappeared altogether and the kids in the front row had to scoot their desks back to avoid being burned as he waved his arms and legs, leaving fiery lines in the air.

The boy after him, Jonsi Huldu from North Oz, was maybe the eeriest person in the room: thin, silvery, and almost see-through, like he was made of mist and would blow away in a decent wind. He had a dark brown bowl cut and enormous gray eyes.

"Hello," he said, swaying slightly on the spot. "My magic is kind of . . . Well . . . I'm sorry."

Ava had just enough time to wonder what he meant when Jonsi opened his mouth and a sound came out. He wasn't singing like Margo—his lips weren't even moving— but something almost like a human voice came pouring out of him. It was high and clear, achingly familiar and yet totally otherworldly. It reminded Ava of the rare morning frosts that touched the desert in winter, or the final petal falling from the last sand rose of the year.

It made her feel utterly, unbearably lonely.

She realized she was rocking in her seat. Plenty of her classmates were doing the same. Others were openly weeping as an avalanche of sorrow filled the room. Even Professor Mulch looked shaken.

Jonsi closed his mouth, and the sound stopped. The weight lifted from Ava's heart. Everyone blinked, sniffing, and Professor Mulch sent around a floating box of tissues.

The white-haired girl who had volunteered for Matthew's demonstration stepped in front of the blackboard next. Her name was Beryl Kralexander, and she was tall and strong-looking, with honey-colored skin and a heavy East Oz accent. She rubbed her knuckles together, smiling a downright nasty smile, and almost at once the slate floor beneath her began boiling and bubbling and a whole army of little ceramic dolls popped out. The dolls ran around the classroom giggling, scratching people's ankles and trying to climb up their legs until Beryl, whose eyes had taken on a reddish glow, stopped making the noise. Instantly, the dolls melted into the floor like they'd never existed, though Ava could still hear faint giggles for a long while afterward.

At last the final student headed for the front: Carmelie Wright. She was also from the South, and her magic took Ava completely by surprise as she cupped her hands together, whispered something into the space between them, then opened her palms to reveal a tiny gingerbread house. All at once the classroom was flooded with the most incredible aroma of cookies, cakes, and caramel. The scent filled Ava's mouth and nose and lungs, and even seemed to be trickling down her ears into her brain. All she wanted was to keep breathing in those delicious smells forever. All she wanted to do was get close to that tiny house.

With a smirk, Carmelie threw the house into her mouth, chomped twice, and swallowed. The smell faded away, and Ava discovered she was on her feet halfway to the blackboard. So were several of her classmates. They all looked around, blinking as they returned to their chairs.

Carmelie flounced back to her desk, exchanging a

high five with a dazed-looking Dorian Cob on the way.

"Fascinating!" yelled Professor Mulch, getting to her feet. "You're certainly an intense group this year. We are going to have fun!"

She returned her chair charm to her antlers, then cleared the blackboard with a slap.

"One final thing before break," she said. "You will have noticed some of the skills you saw today are scary, or disturbing, or even dangerous. So I want to talk to you about wickedness."

Ava could feel the whole class sharpen its attention.

"What *is* wickedness?" Professor Mulch raised an eyebrow, looking around. "Is it something you do or something you are? Something you are born with or something you learn? Is it always bad? And how can you tell?" She pointed to Wolfgang Hex. "Are sparks wicked if they burn you?" Her finger turned to Ava. "Or a cactus if you poke yourself on its spines? Does a person have to choose to be wicked? Or can wickedness work through someone without them even knowing?"

Ava's face went hot as she remembered the destruction her runaway magic had caused at WOW Academy. She hadn't felt wicked when it was happening, but Dean Waterwash had been so certain, even comparing her to famously evil witches like Osmuth Rust, Filbert the Cruel, and Vivienne Morderay. Now Professor Mulch's questions were making her confused all over again. What were the answers? Was she responsible for everything her magic did or not?

"The schools that sent you here," Professor Mulch went on, "think wickedness is like a disease your powers revealed growing inside you. They think Swickwit will crush this wickedness out of you, and that once that happens you will become good forever and ever. They're wrong, of course. The powers you shared today are simply that: your powers. And for the rest of your lives it will be your decision what you do with them. Yes, a few Swickwit graduates grow up to do terrible things. Most do not. You will learn a great deal throughout your years at this school, but I do not believe anything will be as important as this: Who you are is up to you. You always have the final choice."

A heavy, awkward silence filled the classroom.

Professor Mulch threw her hands in the air. "Just some food for thought. Right, break time!"

There was an instant scraping of chairs.

"Be back in your seats in twenty minutes, though!" Professor Mulch called over the chatter and noise. "Or I'll turn you all into apple slices and feed you to the rotting pigeons!"

12

THE PLAN

"Swickwit's not like I expected," said Ava. "Not at all."

It was nighttime, and she and Tinabella were back in their room after dinner. It had been a long first day.

After the morning break, Professor Mulch had given a lecture on magic theory and spellcraft, then they'd had lunch in the Round Room. Ava and Tinabella had kept to themselves again, watching the groups that were already forming among their other classmates. Carmelie had looked over a few times, laughing, but hadn't bothered them again.

When the stairs reappeared, Professor Mulch had announced everyone was free until dinner, then vanished in a burst of dust that made them all sneeze. Most of the other kids had rushed down the stairs, but Tinabella had dragged Ava through the portal door to the library. They'd spent the rest of the afternoon in there, digging into books about the school.

"It doesn't matter what we expected," said Tinabella. "What matters is that we're getting out of here, and that's going to take a seriously brilliant plan."

She shoved the usual mess off her desk and unrolled a

scroll. It was a detailed map of Swickwit, and they might or might not have stolen it. The library rules were hard to decipher.

Ava looked over Tinabella's shoulder and whistled. "It's even bigger than I thought," she said. "What exactly are we looking for?"

"A way out!" snapped Tinabella. "Because this"—she ran her finger all around the edge of the map, where spiky lines marked the hills of broken glass—"and *this*"—she tapped the ring representing the boiling lake—"are not an option. Nobody gets past those, not even the teachers, which means there must be some other way out."

"Like, a secret tunnel or something?" said Ava.

"Exactly."

Ava scrunched her eyebrows together. "Don't you think the grown-ups probably just fly in and out? Gern does. And the dean of West Oz Witch Academy did after she dropped me off."

Tinabella gave her a very sarcastic look. "Oh, sure, let's just *learn to fly*, then! It's not like it's famously the *single hardest kind of magic to do*!"

Ava felt her face get hot. "I didn't know that."

"Well, it is! And I am not staying here that long. I have an injustice to correct and a place at my old school that I should be in. And you've got . . . whatever you said before. There *must* be some other way out. I refuse to accept anything else."

They stayed up late into the night dividing the school into a grid and making their plan to search it piece by piece. It was going to be a lot of work and take up all their free afternoons, but Tinabella pointed out that they shouldn't have to search the whole entire fortress.

"It would be crazy bad luck if the secret exit turned out to be in the last place we looked," she said.

Ava thought there might be something wrong with that logic, especially since they had no guarantees there even *was* a secret exit. But she kept her doubts to herself.

"I bet this will go even quicker than we think," Tinabella said as they were crawling into bed. "Hey, don't forget the light."

Ava got up and turned off the light.

"In fact," Tinabella said into the darkness, "I bet we'll be out of here within a week. Max."

Ava sank into bed, pulling her blanket over her. She wasn't quite as certain about the timeline, but Tinabella seemed certain enough for both of them.

"See you in a week, hopefully," she whispered in her mind to her family, to Peaches, and to the great silver dome of WOW Academy's great hall. "I promise I'll find a way to make everything right."

13

THE SEARCH

In the end, it took a whole entire month before Ava and Tinabella made a real break in the case.

Their days had settled quickly into a rhythm. Every morning they went to class, where they always learned something new. Their second lesson was about how to take the feeling of their core magic and apply it to other things. To Ava's delight, she managed it fairly quickly. It was a massive relief no longer having to worry that her water powers might take over and destroy the school every time she tried a spell. She could still sense nearby water whenever she did magic, but so long as she wasn't connecting with it, she was okay.

Professor Mulch turned out to be a very good teacher. Tinabella mastered hypnotizing frogs on their fourth day, and not long after that Ava discovered she was great at creating floating orbs of light between her hands. Beryl was the best in the class at circles of protection, and Jonsi was such a prodigy at summoning bad dreams that everyone had to put charms over their beds to stop him from practicing on them at night. Poor Crow never managed to do any magic at all.

Ava felt a little sad to be ignoring all their other class-mates, since a few of them, like Margo and Opal and Matthew, seemed nice. Most of the others, though, definitely didn't.

Wolfgang Hex discovered a way to combine his spark power with bubbles and began booby-trapping Nettle Tower whenever he was bored, chuckling to himself as he sent clusters of stinging orbs drifting almost invisibly through the air.

Jadis Frost declared the laboratory was her own personal kingdom and laid a shockingly elaborate curse on the door so only people she liked could get in. So far, three different students had come tumbling back out of the portal wrapped in cocoons of frozen asparagus. The evidence seemed pretty clear that Jadis didn't like anyone very much.

Branwen remained obsessed with her original magical skill of condensing shadows into clouds of despair. She practiced constantly, and even learned to shape the clouds into animals that could run around like the real thing at her command. Her favorite shape was rabbits, for reasons she refused to explain, and the rest of Nettle learned to always check where they stepped to avoid accidental contact with a hopping lump of absolute misery as they went about their day.

And then, of course, there were Carmelie and Dorian, who seemed to grow meaner by the minute. Overall, Ava supposed it was a good thing Tinabella insisted the two of them keep to themselves.

The food at Swickwit continued to surprise Ava—mostly in good ways. Their meals changed often, and she discovered plenty of new dishes she liked. There were mashroot meringues from South Oz, ostridon omelets from East Oz, and burnt buckle burgers from the North. One night, the dining hall offered nothing but ice cream, and they all got to choose from an incredibly long list of flavors: Candleberry, Buttercomb, Fizzing Jasmine, Moon Smoosh, Roasted Applenut, Plorange, and more. There were peculiar flavors, too, like Hot Water, Dodo Breath, Glueberry, and Sour Leech Fizz. Ava didn't try any of those.

Every day after lunch, Ava and Tinabella would head to the next section of fortress marked on their map and continue their search for a secret way out.

It was very weird being ignored by the older students as they made their way around. Cobweb, Cauldron, and Broom kids were everywhere, laughing and arguing and chatting, but every one of them acted like the kids in Nettle green literally didn't exist. It gave Ava an odd, heavy feeling at first, like she'd become a ghost without knowing it. But eventually she got used to it.

Sometimes they spotted Crow wandering the school, too—on his own, of course. Ava felt super sorry for him. His classmates from the past two years were all in Cobweb now, and it must be extra lonely to know so many people who wouldn't acknowledge you. Nobody in their year was talking to him, either, because he was old and awkward and kept failing Nettle, which meant Crow didn't have anyone on his side in the whole entire place. Ava wished more than once she could say something nice to him, but she didn't want to make Tinabella mad.

Day by day, she and Tinabella covered their map in big red Xs, marking every tower, hallway, and dungeon they'd searched. They investigated classrooms full of glowing spiderwebs, storerooms full of rusty knives that whispered when you looked at them, and basements full of oily model trains. They found ghost cats in the greenhouses, a slime fountain in the south courtyard, and four moldy accordions nailed behind a tapestry in the entrance hall. But they didn't find even a hint of a way out.

Not that they were able to search everywhere. Professor Mulch had been right when she'd warned the class there would be plenty of places in Swickwit they couldn't go. Mostly these seemed to be connected with the older kids. By their second week, Ava and Tinabella were pretty certain they'd tracked down the Cobweb and

Cauldron dorms and maybe some of their classrooms—almost nothing on their stolen map was labeled—but what with the hallways turning back on themselves when they tried to get close, or an arch in a certain stairwell constantly portaling them to the nearest empty bathroom, they couldn't be one hundred percent sure.

These unsearchable spots infuriated Tinabella, who declared it wasn't fair and was totally cheating and they shouldn't have to wait until they were older to get access to the whole fortress. Ava didn't understand who exactly Tinabella thought was cheating, but she knew her friend well enough now not to question her when she was angry. Anyway, Ava was just grateful they hadn't stumbled across any spiny scab fleas yet.

Sometimes, for a change, they spent their afternoons back in the library, hunting down every stray scrap of information they could find on Swickwit. This became easier and more fun once Tinabella found a spell that let them search the books by keyword. They tested it out with *secret, tunnel, portal, escape,* and *pillow fort* (just for fun) and dug up some super interesting stuff. None of it turned out to be all that helpful in their current situation, unfortunately, but Ava still enjoyed herself. Tinabella did not. She decided the library was deliberately making things difficult for them and started bringing mountains of books back to their room, insisting they stay up late into the night poring over the pages. But the days and nights slipped by, and for all their hard work they were still no closer to getting out.

They had their first actual breakthrough when they found a secret door out of the fortress while trying to escape an angry horde of Beryl's tiny dolls.

It all started at breakfast, when Beryl took the last slice of toasted bramblemallow cake just as Tinabella spotted it.

"Stop right there!" Tinabella ordered, pointing her fork across the table. "That's mine!"

Beryl shook her snow-white bangs off her forehead, considering the slice in her hand. "Funny, it looks like I got it first."

"But I was *about* to take it! I had eye-dibs!"

"That's not a thing."

"Yes it is, you moose-faced marmot!"

"It's really not. But don't worry—it's okay to be wrong sometimes."

Ava had just enough time to see Tinabella turn a darker purple than the cake before her roommate was charging around the table, hands grabbing and elbows swinging.

Beryl was already tall enough to fend off Tinabella, but she jumped up onto the nearest bench anyway, holding the cake above her head and smiling down with an infuriatingly calm expression.

The whole room was watching as Tinabella stamped her foot in fury.

"Give that back!" she yelled. "Or I'll make you!"

"Okay, seriously? Let it go," called Carmelie from her knot of admirers. "This is totally juvenile."

"What did you just call me?" shouted Tinabella, rounding on her.

"It would be proper to stay out of this," Margo told Carmelie. "This matter is for Beryl and Tinabella to settle without our interference."

"No one asked you," Dorian snapped, flicking a crust of toast at her.

"Hey, don't throw food at people!" said Opal.

"Who put you in charge, fingernail girl?" demanded Branwen.

"Mmm," said Beryl, hopping down and talking loudly over all of them with her mouth full. "This is *so* delicious. This might be the best slice of bramblemallow cake I've *ever* tasted in my life."

Tinabella gave a roar.

Across the room, a grinning Margo lobbed a spoonful

of lemon jam at Dorian. Branwen blocked it with one of her shadow rabbits, and suddenly everyone was on their feet and taking sides.

The magical food fight that followed was short but intense, and amid the bangs and splats and flashes, Tinabella managed to capture what remained of the disputed cake—no one saw how—devouring it with messy glee right in Beryl's face.

With the prize gone, the battle died, and they all spent the rest of breakfast grumbling and cleaning themselves up. Then they went to class.

Everything seemed to go back to normal after that, and Ava had forgotten about the morning's drama by the time she and Tinabella returned to their room to prepare for the afternoon's search. Ava already had the door half-open when she caught the sound of giggling, and by then it was far too late. There was no stopping the avalanche of tiny biting dolls that cascaded out of the room at their feet. They had time to do just one thing: *run*.

Their classmates gasped or cheered (depending on their feelings about Beryl) as Ava and Tinabella bolted down the stairs of Nettle Tower and into the school's twisting halls with an enormous wave of giggling, clawing dolls nipping at their heels.

Tinabella kept herself invisible for most of the chase,

though that didn't deter the dolls. They'd just turned a corner near the llama-haunted auditorium when Ava, whipping her head side to side to see where her friend had gone, spotted the hidden door.

If she hadn't been running for her life, she might never have seen it. The stones on the wall to their left looked smooth and even, but some tiny error in alignment caught her panicked attention, and all at once the outline of a door that was trying not to be there jumped out at her.

Tinabella flickered into sight again, and before she could think or explain, Ava grabbed her by the arm and hurled the two of them at the stone wall. A thud, a click, and one secret spinning door later, they found themselves standing outside the outer walls of the fortress, safe and free under the afternoon sky.

Ava and Tinabella laughed and hugged with excitement at first, and Tinabella even landed some celebratory kicks against the school's stone walls. Then they looked around.

It was a windy day, and the gusts tossed the fog back and forth, exposing their surroundings in shifting, vivid bursts. The ground beneath their feet was crushed black rock, which stretched from the walls out into the fog before dropping off suddenly to the boiling lake.

Tinabella and Ava stood at the top of the slope, looking out, their faces sweating.

"Maybe there's a secret bridge?" Ava said. "Hidden in the mist?"

"Worth a look," said Tinabella, and they set off on a circuit around the fortress.

It was not a fun walk. To their left lay the fog, the boiling water, and an occasional glimpse of the broken-glass hills beyond. To their right, the looming walls of Swickwit, going on and on until eventually they found themselves standing outside the school's enormous front gates.

They were locked, of course. Ava stole Tinabella's idea and gave them a kick, just to see how it would feel, then, remembering her arrival, turned her back on the gates and walked straight out into the fog.

A grumbling Tinabella caught up with her at the Wicked Wagon. They walked around it together, peering through the barred window and wondering aloud what Gern did all year, where he slept (if gargoyles slept), and where he might be now.

"Vacation, I think," said Ava, remembering. "At least that's what he said when he dropped me off."

"Pretty long vacation," said Tinabella.

They returned to the gates and trudged on, continuing

their circuit until they were back at the door where they'd started. A hidden bridge over the lake had been a long shot, but disappointment still settled over them. There was no escape out here. There were only rocks and fog and a good chance of a slippery fall if they weren't careful.

They chucked pebbles into the water for a while, then went back in, even more discouraged than before.

The dolls were gone, happily, and no one said a word about them. But Tinabella never started arguments over breakfast after that.

As the days turned into weeks, it got harder and harder to keep their spirits up.

"We'll find something tomorrow," said Tinabella, pulling Ava out of a disused well that turned out to be full of screaming squidgipedes, not secret passages.

"We have to be close," said Ava, tugging Tinabella through a hallway that had narrowed to one foot wide while they were walking down it.

"We'll be out of here next week for sure," promised Tinabella as they slid down the railing of a spiral stair-case to escape the mummified hyena they'd accidentally released from a rusty suit of armor.

With every location they crossed off their map, the

pressure on the next day grew, until Ava began to wonder how much more she could stand. She still yearned to get back where she belonged, and prove she wasn't wicked, and make her family proud, but after four long weeks it was getting harder and harder to keep believing there must be a secret way out of Swickwit just because she and Tinabella wanted it so much.

Then, at last, when it seemed as if it would truly never happen, they found the room with the clocks.

14

THE CLOCK ROOM

It was Ava's discovery.

They'd been searching a forgotten-looking area on the north side of Swickwit, dusty halls and empty rooms and very little else. It had been ages since they'd even seen any other students, and at times the school had seemed to be stretching and growing around them, twisting back on itself in an unending, pointless maze.

Things had gotten briefly exciting when they spotted a narrow spiral staircase tucked into a dark corner, but all they'd found at the bottom was a grimy storeroom, and disappointment had come slumping back in.

They explored the storeroom anyway. The stone ceiling and walls were filmed with cobwebs, and the light coming through the narrow windows seemed as unhappy to be there as they were. They walked up and down, examining rows of damaged desks, rotting paintings, and broken furniture.

Ava was about to suggest they leave when she spotted an extra-large painting leaning against the far wall. It was as tall as a door and showed an elaborate hunting scene in a forest. Feeling mildly curious, she walked over for a closer look, almost stepping right into a large puddle on the floor beneath the painting.

What was a puddle doing here?

She knelt down. The water was as smooth as glass, and she couldn't resist reaching out a hand to touch it. But right before her finger met the surface something else caught her eye, and she gasped.

"What's up?" said Tinabella, stomping over. She looked down at Ava's discovery. "Oh, wow. A puddle."

"But look!" Ava pointed. "Look at the painting. Then look at the reflection!"

Tinabella looked. She looked again.

"Hey! It's different!"

Ava nodded. In its reflection in the puddle, the center of the painting contained a round, silver doorknob.

Tinabella grabbed eagerly at the canvas. "It's not here," she said. "Why isn't it here?"

"Hang on," said Ava. "Let me see . . ." She got to her feet and stepped backward, keeping her eyes on the reflection as she felt the air behind her. Her hands touched the crackly paint, went the wrong way, tried again . . . and found it.

She gripped the doorknob that wasn't there. She turned.

The whole painting swung open.

Ava spun around, and she and Tinabella stood shoulder to shoulder, staring into a midnight-black opening.

"Wow," said Tinabella.

"Yeah," agreed Ava.

"We finally found something."

"We really did."

Cold, metallic air drifted out of the darkness.

Ava swallowed. "I guess we should . . . go in."

"Mm-hmm," said Tinabella. "You first, though, since you're better at those lights."

So Ava went first, floating three of her glowing orbs above her as she did. They showed a long hallway of glossy black stone and something gold glittering up ahead.

She looked back. "Seems safe enough."

Tinabella followed.

The shiny black hall went on for a full minute, the glimmer of gold growing clearer and brighter until they stepped out into a small square room with an arched ceiling.

Ava sent her lights to float above them, and she and Tinabella took in the room they'd just discovered.

The golden shine, it turned out, was clocks—four enormous grandfather clocks standing in a square in the center of the room and filling the air with a quiet ticking. There was nothing else there. Whatever the secret door was meant to hide, Ava and Tinabella had found it.

The clocks were beautiful, carved and gilded, with glass doors showing lightning-shaped pendulums swinging within. Ava's eyes traveled up and up, admiring, until they snagged on something at the top of the nearest clock. She blinked, feeling her heart begin to pound very fast in her chest.

"So! This is . . . odd," said Tinabella. She turned to Ava, who was shaking her head. "What's the matter with you? You look like a bear trying to get rid of bees."

"The letters!" Ava pointed to the large, curly *W* perched at the top of her clock, then the *N, E,* and *S* decorating the other three. "I saw a clock exactly like these in Dean Waterwash's office at West Oz Witch Academy. I mean *exactly*."

"Okay, great," said Tinabella. "What's your point?"

"What if the *W* stands for *west*? What if these are portals like the library door? What if this clock"—Ava pressed her hands against it—"leads to the other one?"

Tinabella's face went pale. "If you're right, then that would mean this one"—she pointed at the *N* clock—"would lead to North Oz Witch Academy!"

"Exactly!"

"Exactly!"

"Aaah!"

"AAAH!"

They stared at each other in disbelief. After all their hard work, all their planning, all their disappointing searches, they might have just discovered the perfect way to get back where they knew they belonged.

It was an awesome moment.

"Okay, though, wait." Tinabella held up a hand. "We should totally test it. You said you've seen that clock before, so you have to go first."

Ava was beginning to get the tiniest bit sick of constantly having to go first, but Tinabella always had a logical reason why she should, and she couldn't really argue with this one.

"Okay," she said. "Only promise you'll help if I get stuck in there."

"Sure. If you promise to come right back and tell me if it works."

"Deal."

Ava opened the golden *W* clock. The zigzagging pendulum swung back and forth inside, but there was just enough room for her to squeeze in. Taking a deep, excited breath, she pulled the door closed behind her.

For one heartbeat, the world spun upside down. She felt like a coin being flipped.

Then gravity slammed back into place, and she found

herself looking out into Dean Waterwash's empty office.

It took everything Ava had not to scream with happiness as she opened the door and peered around. They had done it! *She* had done it! She was back!

All at once she remembered Tinabella. She tugged the door closed again.

"It worked!" she cried, bursting back into the clock room. "It worked, it worked!"

Tinabella's face blazed with excitement. "North Oz, here I come!" she shouted, running for the *N* clock.

"Be careful!" Ava called after her. "And we should meet back here in five minutes to decide what to do next!"

Ava was just as excited as Tinabella, but she knew they couldn't simply show up at their old schools and expect to be welcomed back with open arms. They would need a whole new plan now to make that happen.

But at least they'd found a way out of Swickwit.

"Fine! Whatever!" Tinabella yelled, yanking open her clock. She jumped in, and Ava got to see her disappear in a green blur between one swing of the pendulum and the next.

Joy filling her up like a spring rain shower, Ava pulled her own door shut again, whooped as she spun, and finally stepped out into the serene, beautiful West Oz office where all her wicked witch troubles had begun.

15

FIVE MINUTES IN WEST OZ

Dean Waterwash's office looked exactly the same.

Afternoon light poured in through the waterfall window, illuminating the paintings, the potted orchids, and the dean's desk and chair. Ava couldn't help running a hand along the nearest bookshelf, just to assure herself it was all real.

She had so many questions.

Why did Swickwit have giant clocks leading into the other witch schools? Did Dean Waterwash know her office clock was part of a portal? (Ava doubted it, or the dean could have just pushed her through it instead of summoning the Wicked Wagon all those weeks ago.)

Why was the clock room at Swickwit hidden in an old forgotten storeroom? Did anyone else at Swickwit know it was there? Had she and Tinabella stumbled across a secret even Warden Pike didn't know?

She had more questions than time, though, so she decided to focus on the one that mattered most: Was there anything she could do right now to make sure WOW Academy would take her back?

She spent two whole precious minutes pacing the office, thinking as hard as she'd ever thought in her life, but had to admit in the end that no, there probably wasn't.

That was okay, though. The hard part was over. She knew how to get here now, and she could come back however many times it took.

Letting herself relax a bit, she decided to be brave and pop her head out into the hall, just to see what she could see.

When she did, she yelped in surprise.

Henry Buffle, her one and only friend from her one and only day at WOW Academy, was sitting on a chair in the hallway.

Henry was just as small as she remembered, and his pale skin and bright pink hair looked even more vivid in his silver school uniform. He looked up at the sound of the door, and Ava saw to her surprise that he was crying. He stopped when he saw her and started goggling instead.

"Hi, Henry!" she said, stepping out to join him.

"Ava? Wh-what were you doing in there? And what are you doing *here*? They sent you away. They said you were w-wicked . . ."

"They were wrong!" said Ava. "Or maybe sort of right, actually, only wicked doesn't mean what they think it does?

I'm still figuring it out. No time to explain about me; why are you out here? And why are you crying?"

Henry's eyes filled with tears again. "I'm being expelled," he mumbled. "I'm no good at magic."

"What? But that duck-and-return thing you do is amazing!"

"That's *all* I can do," Henry said. "After a whole month of classes. That and this." He squeezed his eyes shut and puffed out his cheeks. "See?" He held up one foot, then the other. "The soles of my shoes are a quarter-inch thicker."

"Oh wow," said Ava. "That's . . . really nice."

"No, it's not. It's useless. Dean Waterwash says I'm not living up to the expectations of the school. But she doesn't know what it's like! Sheridan and her friends are always bullying me. Sheridan calls me Little Mr. Duck-Duck. And none of the other kids will talk to me because of her, and because I'm so bad at magic . . ."

Ava's heart ached for the small boy. She would definitely have some words for Sheridan once she was back.

"Professor Ploosh made the decision this morning," Henry went on, "and Dean Waterwash is coming up here right now to expel me. Apparently it's a spell—I'll literally get zoomed home. But I can't face my parents like this!

They have huge expectations. They'll be so, so, SO angry. At everyone."

Ava was just about to ask what he meant when a distant door slammed. Clacking footsteps sounded from down the corridor.

"That's her!" Henry whispered. "That's the dean!" He turned to Ava. "Can you hide me? If I'm not here, she won't be able to do the spell. Please? Just for right now? Just until she's gone and we can figure something out? Please?"

Ava was opening her mouth to say no, and that she had to get out of here before she was caught, too. But then she thought of the secret room waiting back at Swickwit. Could she hide Henry there for a while? It would be a risk. What about Tinabella? What about the secret of Swickwit itself? Would she be giving too much away?

"I don't know . . ." she said, biting her lip.

Then she looked down at Henry Buffle's tear-streaked face, and her heart made up her mind for her.

"Oh, all right, come on," she said, tugging Henry into the office. "Quick!"

The sun was shining straight through the waterfall now, and the stained glass sent blue and silver light dancing off every surface. Henry stared, but Ava shoved him over to the clock.

"Inside," she said, opening the glass front. "I don't know if it can do two people at once, so you go first."

"Wh-where are we going?" Henry asked, squeezing away from the lightning-bolt pendulum as she shut the door. Then he turned, gasped, and disappeared.

Her heart pounding, Ava counted slowly to five, just to be safe. There would be explanations to make to both Henry and Tinabella, but she would deal with them on the other side.

She could hear Dean Waterwash's steps right outside the door.

She saw the doorknob turn as she stepped into the clock.

She caught one brief glimpse of liquid-silver robes . . . and spun away into the dark, feeling triumphant.

She had successfully snuck into her old dean's office. She had rescued a friend. And once she and Henry put their heads together, she was certain they would find a way to win back their places at WOW Academy. Her world was returning to how it was supposed to be, and soon she would prove herself to her family, her teachers and classmates, and all of Oz.

At long last, everything was finally going right.

The spinning settled. Beaming, she opened the door of the shining clock . . .

. . . and stepped out into absolute chaos.

16

TRULY WICKED

The secret clock room had become a disaster zone.

The glowing orbs Ava had left floating overhead spun dizzyingly as poison-green moths the size of pillows batted them around the ceiling.

The clock that led north was lying on its side, its open glass door in splinters as an enormous black bear climbed out, roaring and slashing at the air with razor-sharp claws.

Ava had to jump out of the way as a cloud of squawking ravens whipped past her, zigzagging across the chamber floor in pursuit of something invisible.

Invisible, but noisy.

"Helllllp!" screamed Tinabella, her cries echoing off the walls. "Help help helllllp!" She flickered into sight for a moment, panting, and waved at Ava. "Do something! Don't know—how long—keep running!"

The horde of ravens swooped and she disappeared again, the slap of her feet joining the birds' screeches and the bear's thundering roars.

Poor Henry Buffle was trapped in a corner, ghost

white and trembling as he faced down a snapping, red-eyed wolf. Each time it lunged, Henry ducked, pushing the wolf back to where it had started. But that was only a temporary defense, and the wolf was getting angrier with every attempt.

Ava stood beside the *W* clock, totally overwhelmed, trying to think.

What in Oz had happened here?! Where had all these animals come from?

Most important, what could she do to save her friends? There wasn't a drop of water or a plant to be seen, and the little things she'd learned in class so far wouldn't do much against ravens or wolves or angry bears.

She was just bringing her hands together to conjure more lights, hoping to maybe distract the animals if she made enough of them, when a shout came echoing down the hallway and Warden Pike appeared at a full run.

He skidded into the room, cried something in a wild, crunchy-sounding language, and clapped both hands together over his head.

There was a searing flash of light, and everything stopped.

Ava felt herself go rigid, exactly like when Margo had demonstrated her singing on their first day of class.

Tinabella flickered back into view, sweat plastering her bangs to her face. Henry and the wolf stood frozen almost nose to nose. Caught midflight, the moths and ravens dropped to the floor with heavy thumps. Even the lights overhead stopped spinning.

"What," said Warden Pike into the sudden stillness, "is going on here?"

Ava watched as he strode slowly past the moths and ravens to the center of the room, his eyes moving side to side, taking in every detail. He seemed to be radiating power; Ava could see it flickering around him like dark fire.

Warden Pike raised both arms and began chanting under his breath. A rumbling filled the air, growing deeper and louder until, with a crunch and a roar, the bear disappeared back through the ruined North Oz clock.

The wolf began to follow, howling as it slid backward across the floor and through the shattered glass. Then it twisted at the last second, clamping its terrible jaws around the clock frame, holding on with its red eyes still fixed on Henry.

Warden Pike chanted louder, sending the moths and ravens tumbling through the door around it, ramping up the magical pressure until finally, with another crunch and a furious howl, the wolf slipped through. What was left of the clock door slammed shut, and a ringing silence fell over the secret chamber.

Warden Pike clicked his fingers, and Ava found she could move again. She saw Tinabella and Henry sag with relief.

"You three," said Warden Pike, pointing to the floor in front of him. "Here. Now."

Ava stepped forward, feeling sick. She hated being in trouble more than anything in the world, and they were clearly in big, *big* trouble. Even worse, she could feel a wild cackle building, just like the one she'd let loose after destroying the WOW Academy great hall.

Henry shuffled over to stand beside her, his eyes huge behind his flop of bright pink hair, and the terror on his face helped Ava swallow down her cackle. She felt terrible. She'd promised him he would be safe here. They were only supposed to be hanging out for a bit, brainstorming ways to help him stay at WOW Academy while they waited for Dean Waterwash to leave her office again. Instead, she'd brought him directly into a nightmare.

What would happen to Henry now?

Tinabella stomped over last, looking like a walking thundercloud of anger and frustration.

Warden Pike glared down at them for a long moment, then pointed to Ava. "You. Where did you go, and what happened when you got there? I want every detail."

Ava told him.

"So no one saw you?" Warden Pike's glowing white eyes burned into hers. "Apart from this boy, no one saw you? And you closed the clock after you? And left no trace?"

"Y-yes. No. Yes, no one saw me. I closed the door. I didn't change anything."

Warden Pike let out a breath. "All right." He turned to Tinabella. "You went North, that is obvious. What happened?"

Tinabella knotted her arms together over her chest. "I ended up in Headmaster Mossfoot's office," she answered. "I recognized it from before. It's made of pine logs and granite, and there's gold everywhere. I wanted to find out who set me up and got me sent here, so I tried casting the keyword spell on his desk. This bundle of letters flew out of a drawer. They all had my name on them, and the top one was from Mr. Pheasant, my father's archenemy. He was thanking Headmaster Mossfoot for his help making his son Timmybob the best new student in the school."

Tinabella was talking faster and faster. "But you know who else he thanked? *My father.* I read the whole thing in the other letters. Mr. Pheasant offered to give my father the Blue Cedar Waterfall if he kept me out of school so Timmybob could be the best. My father's been obsessed with that waterfall his whole life, so he said yes! Then he and Headmaster Mossfoot decided the easiest way to get me out of school was to have me declared wicked during my entrance test. Everyone *knew* I wasn't wicked, and my own greedy, two-faced, selfish father agreed to have me flown off here anyway! All so he could own one more waterfall!" She rubbed her face with her hands. "And I totally should have kept the letters as proof, but I was so mad I tore them into little pieces. That was when those animals came out of the walls. I barely made it back through the clock, and, well, you saw what happened: They followed me."

Ava became aware her mouth was hanging open. She'd had no idea Tinabella was dealing with so much drama and family trouble back home. She could barely understand the details, let alone wrap her mind around the idea of being part of a family that acted like that.

Her roommate had been going through a lot.

Warden Pike shook his head. "I am sorry about your father," he said. "But it was foolish to touch anything. Headmaster Mossfoot booby-traps his office when he is not in it. The heads of the South and East schools do, too. They are all careful and suspicious." He turned to Ava. "You were lucky. The deans of West Oz Witch Academy place too much faith in their own sense of superiority to suspect they may be vulnerable."

He gestured to the room. "These clocks are two-way doors, sent as gifts to the other schools hundreds of years ago to enable the warden of Swickwit to spy on them unobserved. They are an essential part of how we have kept our staff and students safe: by keeping a close eye on those who would take it all away if they knew the truth."

Ava tried to picture generations of Swickwit wardens prowling in and out of all the other schools, but they all looked like Warden Pike in her head. She blinked, glancing up at the real one. How old was he, anyway?

"Headmaster Mossfoot will know his office security has been triggered," Warden Pike went on, looking back at the wreck of the North Oz clock. "Though hopefully the animals will have done enough damage to keep any suspicion away from how the intruder got in.

"It is very lucky for you I always know the instant someone enters this room. It is less lucky I was away from the school when the alarm sounded. Another few minutes, and I might have truly been too late. But what were you doing down here in the first place?"

Ava decided there was no point trying to hide anymore. "We've been looking for a way out," she said. "Like

a secret tunnel under the lake or something. We're just—
we don't think we belong here."

"You were looking for a way out," repeated Warden
Pike slowly. "You were willing to put all of Swickwit in
danger for your own benefit. Well, I am glad to know
where you two stand."

"No!" said Ava. "That's not—"

Warden Pike silenced her with a look.

"And to kidnap another child back with you on top of
everything? That is truly wicked. I am almost impressed."
He turned his attention to Henry. "What is your name?"

"H-Henry B-Buffle."

"Henry Buffle," said Warden Pike. "Well, it looks like
you are no longer the only West Oz witch here, Miss
Heartstraw. Welcome to your new home, Mr. Buffle."

"What?" Henry went faintly green. "I—I can't stay
here! Please! You have to let me go. My parents— If they
don't hear from me every week, they get—"

"I promised!" Ava said over him. "I promised he could
go back when the coast was clear!"

"That," said Warden Pike, "was a mistake. Anyone
who learns the Swickwit secret must stay until they have
graduated Broom level. I told you that when you arrived.
No student leaves this fortress until they are old and wise
enough to be trusted, and any trust I had in you two"—his

eyes burned into Ava and Tinabella—"is currently dead and buried. We will have to see if you ever manage to earn it back."

Tinabella folded her arms again and kicked at the floor.

Ava felt as sick as if she'd eaten a vat of Sour Leech Fizz ice cream.

She was in trouble in the middle of a mess again, even though—just like every time before—she hadn't meant to do anything wrong. She still believed her intentions were important, but these disasters really *did* keep happening. With so many different grown-ups telling her she was being wicked, the question had to be asked: How many accidentally wicked things could one person do and still be good?

"I'm sorry," she mumbled. "What, um, happens now?"

"Now I escort the three of you out of this room," answered Warden Pike. "Which is, by the way, the one and only secret passage out of Swickwit. Then I make utterly certain neither you nor any other student is able to find it again."

The warden marched their little group away from the clocks, back through the storage basement, up the spiral stairs, and all the way to the foot of Nettle Tower's stairs. Henry cried silently the whole time, and Ava had to dig her nails into her palms not to join him.

She and Tinabella had come *so close* to making everything right. They had found their way home. They had almost done it. Only now their escape route would be cut off forever. Now they were truly trapped. And thanks to her, so was poor little Henry.

Everything, absolutely everything, was going wrong.

17

A STRANGE TWIST

Ava slept badly that night. She and Tinabella had had to sit through two long, awful lectures from Warden Pike and Professor Mulch, then been sent to bed without any supper like naughty children in a fairy tale.

She heard Tinabella tossing all night, too, but when she finally woke in the morning, her roommate was already gone. Ava washed, dressed, and stepped into the hall, where the first thing she noticed was that the door across from them had changed.

The top nameplate still read CROW BACKPATCH (EAST), but a new one under it read HENRY BUFFLE (WEST). Ava smiled a little, picturing the two shy boys sharing a room. Hopefully they would get along. And it would certainly be nice having another friend around now that she was trapped here forever . . .

Her smile dropped. Henry was trapped here, too—because of her. She hadn't meant for that to happen. She had just wanted to help. She'd made a mistake, but it had been an honest one, and an honest mistake could never be really, truly wrong.

Right?

Ava got another surprise as she entered the Round Room: Instead of waiting for Ava on their usual bench, Tinabella was sitting with the popular kids on the opposite side of the room, chatting away happily to . . . Carmelie.

Ava stopped in her tracks, blinking. Then she understood. She'd been too upset to realize it earlier, but she and Tinabella could begin making friends with their classmates now that their escape plans were over. It looked like Tinabella had already made a good start.

She scanned the room for Henry, but he wasn't there. Crow was, eating by himself as usual. He gave Ava a shy smile as she gathered her fruit and toast. She smiled back and went to join Tinabella.

The chattering group looked up as she reached them.

"What?" said Carmelie, smoothing a green feather woven into her hair.

"Hi." Ava stood there, awkwardly holding her breakfast. "Can I, um, sit with you?"

Jadis and Wolfgang giggled. Tinabella looked up at Ava. She had a green feather, too.

"It's already kind of crowded," Tinabella said.

"Oh," said Ava.

Tinabella didn't say anything more, just sat there looking at Ava. They all looked at Ava.

"I guess I'll . . . eat somewhere else, then?" she said.

"Love that idea," said Carmelie.

Ava caught Tinabella's eye. "See you at break?"

Tinabella shrugged. "Maybe."

Ava headed for their old bench, her insides churning. What was going on? Had she missed something the night before? Why was her roommate treating her like a stranger?

Why was everything changing so fast?

Ava finally located Henry as they all trooped into the classroom, where her little friend was standing up front by the blackboard, dressed in a green Nettle uniform, looking terrified.

"We have a new student," shouted Professor Mulch as everyone took their seats. "Henry Buffle here is a late arrival from West Oz." The class oohed. "Yes, apparently his wickedness was a little slow in showing itself. But he's here now! Mr. Buffle, please demonstrate your magic for the class."

"Wh-what?" Henry clearly hadn't been told what was coming.

"Now, please!"

Henry gulped. "Um, okay. I, uh, I need someone to throw something at me."

"What?" yelled Professor Mulch.

"I need someone to throw something at me!"

"On it!" Beryl shouted, and she hurled her spell book.

Henry ducked. The spell book returned to Beryl's hand.

Carmelie sat up, a grin spreading across her face. Jadis did the same, and Wolfgang, and Dorian. Next second the whole class was hurling objects at him: spell books, pencils, hair ties, even a few desks. Henry ducked and dodged, popping up and down until he was pink and panting. Even Tinabella joined in the fun. Ava did not.

"All right, all right!" boomed Professor Mulch. "That's quite enough."

Margo put her hand in the air. "I do not understand, Professor. What is wicked about that magic? It looks like a perfectly practical skill to me."

"Appearances can be deceiving!" Professor Mulch warned. "Oh, I almost forgot! Henry, we need to send you through the void. Just a quick trip to scrape off any curses or astral nasties you may be carrying."

To Ava's surprise, Henry went as white as a lizard skull. "Curses? N-no, I'm not cursed. And besides, they, um, they already did that void thing at my other school."

"Oh! Well, that's all right, then!" Professor Mulch magicked up a desk for Henry and he sat down, clearly grateful to be out of the spotlight.

Ava peered at him. She was almost certain Henry had just told a lie.

"Right!" Professor Mulch smacked the blackboard. "Eyes and brains up here! And no, Opal, I do not mean literally! Let's not have a repeat of last week just because you learned how." The class laughed. Opal grinned. "Today we are jumping ahead to see how you all do trying out a Cobweb skill. Why? Because I feel like it. The skill is elemental magic, and we are going to start with water."

Ava jolted up, every alarm inside her ringing.

She hadn't connected directly with water once since that first day of class. It was way too dangerous. What if she lost control like at WOW Academy? What if she ruined everything—again?

Well, muttered a voice at the back of her head, *you did just ruin Henry's life without using water magic. Maybe the power was never the problem. Maybe it was always you.*

Ava pushed the voice away and tuned back in to the lesson. If she kept her head down and pretended to be really bad at this, maybe, just maybe, she could hold on to her secret and keep her classmates safe.

Professor Mulch was screaming with her hands over

her eyes again, and this time a long stone trough appeared at the front of the classroom. Another shriek, and water came pouring out of thin air, filling the trough in seconds. Ava shivered.

"Now, then," bawled Professor Mulch. "Everybody but Miss Heartstraw pay close attention!"

What?

Oh no.

Everyone turned to look at Ava, who felt as though her whole body had burst into flame.

Dorian raised his hand. "Why doesn't she have to pay attention, Professor?"

"Because she doesn't need to. And you know why, don't you, Ava?"

Ava frantically shook her head. She couldn't handle another disaster. Not so soon.

Professor Mulch gave an exasperated sigh.

"Great worms below, there's no use denying the truth, little cabbage! I spotted it the moment you performed that farce with the cactus at the beginning of the year. You're a born water witch, girl!"

18

A NEW TALENT

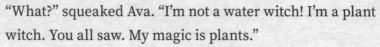

"What?" squeaked Ava. "I'm not a water witch! I'm a plant witch. You all saw. My magic is plants."

"The water *in* plants, girl," barked Professor Mulch. "You did a decent job hiding it with that cactus, but you can't fool me. I assume you've been avoiding your real skills because you caused some sort of watery catastrophe at your first school?"

Ava opened her mouth to deny it, but over in the corner Henry murmured, "Woo yeah."

"Aha!" said Professor Mulch. "You saw it happen, then, Mr. Buffle?"

Henry went bright crimson as the whole class turned to him. He met Ava's eyes, looking mortified.

"Um, y-yes, sorry," he said. "There was—Ava did, um . . . It was impressive."

"It would be!" Professor Mulch squinted at Ava. "Born elemental witches are rare, and usually very powerful. That means there's nothing I can teach Miss Heartstraw at this level. As for the rest of you"—she turned her attention to the other students—"here is how to start connecting with this difficult element. Watch closely."

Flustered, but deeply relieved she wouldn't have to participate, Ava spent the class thinking about what she'd just learned while Professor Mulch demonstrated how to weave patterns into the water's surface, pull droplets up into glistening spheres, and peel off paper-thin layers to float through the air like leaves.

The power that had gotten her into this mess, the power she'd been avoiding this whole time, was . . . special? Did that mean she should start using it, even if it scared her? Had she been wrong about her magic being wicked?

Had she been wrong about everything from the start?

Henry spent their break time hiding in his room, and Tinabella was busy with Carmelie again, so Ava stayed in the classroom flipping through the notes that had written themselves into her spell book. It was strange to see her own powers described in detail. Water magic just seemed perfectly obvious to her.

After the break, Professor Mulch called students up one by one to see what they could do. Most of them, including Crow and Henry, couldn't affect the water at all. Carmelie created one very small wave that flopped over the side, soaking her shoes. Branwen managed to pull a few floating drops into the air, earning a shout of encouragement from Professor Mulch.

"Right! Everyone had a go?" the professor hollered when they were done. "Who wants to see how a real water witch does it? Miss Heartstraw, come on up!"

Ava, whose mind had been wandering, jumped like a startled camel lizard.

Demonstrate her water powers in front of the class? She wasn't ready! She'd only just learned they might not be evil. What if she still didn't have control?

"I'm not sure—" she began, but Professor Mulch boomed down her objections, and Ava found herself standing up front, every eye in the class watching and ready to judge.

She looked for her friends, but Henry was nervously scooting back his desk in one corner, and Tinabella was looking on with complete indifference in the other. Neither reaction had her brimming with confidence.

But it looked like this was happening.

Taking a deep breath, Ava reached cautiously for the power she'd been ignoring all these weeks.

Instantly, water roared through her. This was nothing like her first day with the cactus. This was like stepping into the waterfall in Dean Waterwash's office window, only real. She breathed through it, getting her bearings, hoping she wasn't about to destroy all of Nettle Tower. The power felt stronger than she remembered . . . but to her surprise, she felt stronger, too. Was that because she'd been studying other kinds of magic?

Whatever the reason, it felt great.

Ava held a hand out to the trough, and the surface ruffled, shifting back and forth in waves.

"Wow, amazing," muttered Carmelie. Dorian laughed.

Ava ignored them, reaching out for that new feeling of strength and magical possibility. Goose bumps covered her arms and legs.

It was time to see what she could do.

She began by trying out the skills Professor Mulch had demonstrated: the spikes, the wobbling spheres, the paper-thin slices off the surface. They were all easy, so she made up a few more on the spot. A smile grew on her face as the water stacked itself effortlessly into neat clear blocks, then separated into thousands of minuscule droplets shifting under her fingers like sand.

She held perfectly still for a moment, feeling poised on the edge of something glorious in her mind.

Then she let herself go for it.

The watching class gasped as she pulled the entire pool of water out of the trough and sent it spinning around the room. She whooshed it over the other kids' heads, making them duck, then broke it into a dozen long threads corkscrewing in every direction before swooping it into a huge ball and letting it crash down from the writhing root ceiling, drenching her and splashing the whole front row.

There were shrieks of outrage, but Ava was already pulling the water back off them, even drying out Carmelie's shoes for her, just because she could. She stood there, perfectly dry again, the water spiraling around her head, and laughed.

She laughed because this was easy. Because this felt like home. Because this was—

"Enough!"

Professor Mulch strode forward, and Ava felt control of the water snap from her to the teacher. One wave of the professor's hands, and all the water was back in the trough.

Ava realized she was shaking.

"Thank you, Miss Heartstraw," Professor Mulch hollered. "Very inspiring. No, stay where you are for a moment. The rest of you, remember that elemental magic is Cobweb-level work, so don't expect to be doing anything like that for a good while. Frankly, I'm shocked anyone but Miss Heartstraw was able to connect with the water at all, but it's always nice to be surprised as a teacher, especially after ninety-seven long, hard years."

She glared at the class until they gave her a round of applause.

"Thank you, thank you. And speaking of ninety-seven years, I'm pooped! Review your notes for the remainder of class and then we'll call it a day."

Professor Mulch pulled Ava over to the window while the rest of the class opened their spell books.

"I thought maybe you needed that, Heartstraw," she said in a low voice. "A chance to be seen in a different light. I knew you'd impress—that's why I pushed you. Only don't show off so much next time. Discovering your own strength is worth celebrating, but not so it makes anybody else feel small."

"Oh," said Ava. "Sorry, I didn't—"

"And I want you to know I'm no longer angry about the clock room," Professor Mulch went on, as though Ava hadn't spoken. "I know you've been resisting settling in here. You're not the first; I see it every year. Though you certainly did come closer to getting out than I've ever heard of! My wish for you is that you really try to make this place your home now. We all want you to succeed. Just maybe don't put the whole school at risk the next time you want an adventure."

She poked Ava in the ribs, almost poked her in the eye with her antlers, and went to clean off the blackboard.

Ava stayed beside the window, glad to have a second to sort out how she was feeling.

Had she really been showing off? She hadn't meant to. It had just felt so good to dig into her power like that. Not to mention plain old fun.

And if there was going to be fun sometimes at Swickwit, could she maybe learn to like it here? Could she do what Professor Mulch had asked? Could she really learn to think of this place as her home?

Did she even have a choice?

Outside, a curl of wind pushed through the fog, revealing a glimpse of dark, bubbling water.

Ava went very still as a startling thought fluttered to life in her mind.

The boiling lake and hills of broken glass were Swickwit's ultimate barriers, a constant reminder that even though the horrible School for Wicked Witches was a cover story, they really were all trapped on this island.

Only what if one of those barriers wasn't a problem anymore?

What if Ava's elemental powers might be the key to a new way out?

What if she still had a razor-thin chance to escape?

19

A NEW TEAM

Whispers and glances followed Ava as she rushed into the Round Room after class. Tinabella was already heading down the stairs, Carmelie and Dorian at her heels.

"Tinabella!" Ava shouted, her new plan burning in her like the desert sun at noon.

Tinabella looked up. "What?"

"We have to talk!"

Carmelie snorted. "She's probably wondering why you're not congratulating her on her drippy powers."

"Yeah," said Dorian. "I mean, who shows off like that?" He raised an eyebrow at Ava. "Other people are good at stuff, too, you know."

"Give me a second," Tinabella told them. "This won't take long."

She crossed to an empty bench near the library door and sat, folding her arms.

"What's up?"

Ava dropped down beside her, her excitement bubbling over. "I have an idea! I can—I mean—I'm almost certain I can get us out of here! We can maybe still escape!"

"Oh," said Tinabella.

"It's because of the water. I thought my powers might be too wicked to really use before, but now it's okay, and I think I can use them to get us across the boiling lake!"

"Cool," said Tinabella.

"I mean, there's still the glass hills to get past somehow, and then walking all the way home, and that might be tricky since you're going north and I'm going west, but maybe we can get rides, and—"

"Stop." Tinabella held up a hand. "Just stop."

Ava stopped.

"Obviously you haven't noticed, but things are different now," Tinabella said. She raised her chin. "I don't want to leave Swickwit."

Ava gaped at her.

"As far as I'm concerned, I totally succeeded yesterday. I made it back to North Oz like I said I would, and I found out what got me sent here. Okay, there were wolves and bears and whatever, but I got my answers. That was all I wanted."

Ava blinked. "But what about revenge on Timmybob? What about your rightful place at your old school? What about 'Not North Oz? Say No Way'?"

"Oh, I am *over* that school. And I'll get my revenge someday." The old fire flickered in Tinabella's eyes.

"That's exactly why I'm *choosing* Swickwit. I'm going to become the greatest witch Oz has ever seen. Then I'll go back north and make all of them regret it, starting with my greedy father." She examined her fingernails. "So yeah, I'm staying, and from now on I'm gonna use my afternoons to level up my skills. Carmelie and Dorian want me to join this Cursed Cookie Cutters baking club they're starting. Carmelie obviously has this intense connection with gingerbread, and she's certain there's, like, major power in magic baked goods."

"Oh," said Ava.

"Which means I'm not gonna keep running around the school with you looking for a way out. I'm done with that. It's over."

"Okay."

"And can I be super honest?" Tinabella leaned in close. "Ava, you're, well, pretty weird. Sorry, but it's true. I only really hung out with you because I thought you could help me get home. But I don't want that anymore, so you understand why I'm gonna be spending my time with cooler people from now on, right?"

Ava found herself going through her second emotional whiplash of the day as she suddenly saw the girl beside her in a whole new light.

Tinabella, it turned out, was kind of mean.

"I mean, obviously we're still roommates," Tinabella went on, completely missing the hurricane of feelings crossing Ava's face. "So we'll talk and stuff. We just won't be spending every minute together anymore."

Ava turned her head away. The Round Room was emptying out, and she spotted Henry sitting awkwardly by himself on the opposite side of the stairs.

An unexpected lightness floated through the weight in her chest, followed by a zing of hope.

"Okay," she said. "Sure. I understand."

It was Tinabella's turn to blink.

"It was just an idea," Ava went on, getting to her feet. "Sorry to bother you." She turned and walked away. "Have fun baking stuff!"

Henry looked up gratefully as Ava sat down beside him.

"Hi," he said. "I hope you didn't get in too much trouble yesterday. And I'm so, so sorry for telling the teacher about your WOW Academy testing. I feel awful."

Across the room, a puzzled-looking Tinabella led Carmelie and Dorian down the stairs.

Grinning a little, Ava turned to Henry. "It's fine," she said. "Forget it. And I'm super sorry for getting you trapped here. If I'd known Warden Pike was going to catch us in the clock room, I never ever would have pushed you through. Anyway, listen." She pitched her voice low. "Do you want to get back? To WOW Academy?"

Henry's eyes widened. "Yes!" he said. "Well, only if I'm not going to be expelled right away, and I start doing better in class, and Sheridan and her friends leave me alone."

"That's all important," Ava said, nodding. "But none of it matters unless we can get away from Swickwit first. And I think we can."

"Didn't that warden guy say the clocks were the only way out?"

"This is new. I didn't know it was safe to use my water powers until today." She leaned in close. "If I'm right, I should be able to get us past the—"

"Excuse me, what are you two whispering about?"

Ava and Henry whipped their heads around to find Crow standing in front of them.

"Just . . . West Oz," Ava covered quickly. "Memories, you know. Of West Oz. Where we're both from."

"Oh," said Crow. "Sorry. I thought I heard you saying something about getting away from Swickwit."

Henry squeaked like a baby desert chipmunk. Ava went very still.

"Nooo," she said. "No, you must have misheard."

"Shoot." Crow hung his head. "I was gonna ask if I could come with you."

Ava stared at the older boy.

"You were?" Henry asked. "Why?"

Crow stared moodily around. "Lots of reasons, I guess. I've been stuck in Nettle for a few years now. I make friends and then they move on to Cobweb and never talk to me again. Professor Mulch has to keep magicking my uniforms bigger so the sleeves fit. Stuff like that keeps adding up in my head, and lately I've been thinking: *Crow, maybe this place just isn't for you.*"

Ava swallowed. "Okay, um, where *is* the place for you, then? Henry and I would be going west if we were trying to leave—which I'm not saying we are! But you're from East Oz, right? In the opposite direction?"

"That's okay, I don't have any family back east. Or friends. Or anyone at all."

"Oh. I'm so sorry," said Ava.

Crow shrugged. "I've never known any different. But it does get lonely sometimes. At least I think that's what that feeling is. Anyway, West Oz sounds nice. I'll go there with you if that's okay."

Maybe she was just tired after all the excitement of the morning, but Ava suddenly wanted to cry.

She wouldn't, of course. She hadn't made it this far without crying to give in now.

"I guess you could come west with us," she said slowly.

"If we were trying to leave," added Henry.

"Which we're not."

Crow moved his dark eyes between them.

"I know I don't have the most brains around here," he said. "But it seems like maybe you are."

There were three heartbeats of silence, then Ava felt her resolve break.

"Okay, fine, we are," she said. "And sure, you can come with us."

An unexpectedly beautiful smile lit up Crow's face. "Thanks," he said. "Thank you."

"Only we really shouldn't be talking about it here," said Ava. "Let's go outside."

"Like to the courtyards?" asked Crow.

"Like beside the lake. I found a way."

She realized as she made the invitation that they would be shaping two bricks with one mallet: The lake would provide a listener-proof place to plan, plus it would give her a chance to test out her powers, since if she couldn't make the boiling water do what she wanted they had no chance of escaping anyway.

"Wow!" said Crow. "I always wanted to go on a field trip!" He beamed. "I haven't been outside the walls since I got here."

Henry was nervous about leaving Nettle Tower, so

Crow and Ava promised to let him walk between them the whole way. Ava had almost forgotten it was his very first day at the school.

They set out through the library, then took the many twists and turns to the secret exit. Henry kept cowering every time older kids in their copper, gray, and black uniforms walked by, which made Ava realize she hardly even noticed them anymore. They were just part of the school, things to be avoided when they crossed your path, like the wandering stone columns and Wolfgang's bubble-spark booby traps and the moldy life-size paper horse that galloped endlessly up and down the long picture gallery.

Crow oohed as they stepped out into the fog and immediately ran around trying to see everything. Henry stayed close as Ava led the way to the lake.

"I always wondered if there are fish in here," said Crow, dashing up and crouching to stare into the bubbling surface. "Or maybe giant lobsters?"

Ava raised her eyebrows at him.

"Can we please hurry?" asked Henry. "It's sort of scary out here."

"Sure," said Ava. "Just give me a second." She was feeling more than a little nervous. Everything depended on her being able to do this next part. Their whole future was in her hands.

She reached out, found her power and the water, and carefully made contact . . .

It took Ava a moment to realize she was laughing. Not cackling, thank goodness, just regular, happy laughing. The lake felt amazing! She'd been worried connecting with the boiling water might be painful, but instead it hummed and fizzed, tickling the back of her head like a million dancing ladybugs.

She pulled a geyser from the surface in front of them, sending it hissing high into the air. Henry shouted and jumped behind Crow, but Ava was already arcing the water over the waves, weaving it into shimmering shapes. For the next few minutes she practiced, gathering and releasing, testing her limits, until she felt certain she could make the lake do anything she wanted.

"Whew!" Ava wiped her forehead as she finally stepped back, her hands shaking. An ache in her bones told her she'd probably overdone it a bit, but she was pleased.

"It works," she reported. "I can get us across."

"Hooray!" Crow gave her a double high five.

"Okay, but—but *how*, exactly?" Henry said. "Isn't that water still super hot, even if you can move it around?"

Ava held up a hand. "No worries. We're going to ride across in the Wicked Wagon."

"The what?"

Ava explained, then shared her plan. "It's right where Gern left it, and as far as I know he's still on vacation. We'll get inside, then I'll bring the water up and have it float us across. That wagon is strong; it'll totally protect us."

"And then we'll be free!" Crow whooped.

"Yeah!" Ava grinned. "Well, we'll have done our first big step, anyway. We still need a plan to get past those."

She reached out with her power again, clearing a line through the fog so they could see the hills of broken glass. They were a scary sight from here. They would be terrifying up close.

"Oh, yikes," said Henry. "So much for that."

Ava felt her happiness start to fade. Was Henry right? Neither of her friends was any good at magic, and she sure didn't know any spells that could get them over those glittering hills.

"That's okay," said Crow. "I can do that part."

Ava gaped at him. "What are you talking about?" she asked.

Crow's calm smile widened. "I've been daydreaming about leaving since the second time I flunked Nettle," he said. "I always knew I could get past the glass hills, only the lake was in the way."

"But *how*?" Ava challenged. "I've never even seen you do magic!"

"I know. But I can." Crow tilted his head at Ava's look of disbelief. "Henry and I are trusting you about the water, right? Maybe you could trust me about this."

Ava couldn't think of anything to say to that. She released the fog, feeling real hope blossoming inside her again.

"Okay," she said. "So . . . we've got a plan?"

The three of them stood together on the shore of the boiling lake, exchanging smiles. Not one person had escaped Swickwit in a thousand years, but they were going to give it their very best shot.

"What now?" asked Henry.

"Now we'd better tell Crow the real story behind how you got here," said Ava. "Just so we're all on the same page. Then we get to work."

20

A NEW HOPE

They spent a full week getting ready. Crow didn't think there was that much to talk about, but Henry worried over everything, and Ava was too aware this was her one final chance at escape to leave anything up in the air.

They held their meetings under a table in a corner of the library, cozying in with snacks and pillows stolen from nearby armchairs. It was actually quite fun. Also safe, since the three of them were now officially the least popular kids in Nettle. Tinabella's friendship with Carmelie had shifted the social dynamics, and one by one all the others had fallen under their spell. Even Ava's status as a newly revealed water witch hadn't done her any favors. In fact, it seemed to have made her reputation worse.

Finally, after plenty of work, the three friends' plans were set.

They would leave at night through the library. Escaping Nettle Tower by night had seemed impossible at first, since the stairs always vanished, and the portal doors would only open between the end of class and bedtime. Then one afternoon Henry cleared his throat in their library pillow pile, looking cautiously pleased with himself.

"So I had this idea," he said. "Remember the clock room, Ava?"

Ava smiled. "The secret chamber under the school where we got attacked by bears and wolves and giant moths from North Oz? Sorry, doesn't ring a bell."

"It sounds so amazing." Crow sighed. "I wish I could have seen it."

"Well," said Henry. "Those clocks were portals, right?"

Ava shrugged. "Warden Pike said they were two-way doors, but it's probably the same thing."

"Great. And do you remember when he was zooming all the animals back and that wolf got stuck and the portal wouldn't close until it was through?"

"Of course."

"So amazing," repeated Crow.

"So I was thinking about that the other day: What if it's, like, a rule that portals can't close while there's something alive in them? You know, as a safety measure or something?"

"Ooh, that would be smart thinking," said Crow.

"I guess that could make sense," Ava said, beginning to wonder where Henry was heading with this.

"Okay. So." Henry's knee was jiggling and his cheeks

were turning almost as pink as his hair. "I was wondering if we might be able to do something like that with our door that leads to the library? Obviously, we can't use a person or animal, but there are plenty of other things that are alive, and the other day Crow and I were walking past that slime fountain . . ."

"And you got some on your robes!" said Crow. "That was bad luck, buddy."

"I, um, did it on purpose," Henry said. "Then I smeared the slime across the library doorframe when we were heading back to bed. I got back up once I was sure everyone else was asleep, and, well, basically . . . it worked. The library door opened in the middle of the night. I could walk right through."

Ava stared at him.

"The only bad thing is I don't think we can wipe the slime off until daytime in case the portal slams shut or something. But hopefully no one will spot it for a while."

Ava continued staring.

"So, yeah . . . Um, what do you think?"

Ava stared at Henry for another full ten seconds.

"Are you telling me," she said at last, leaning in close, "that you figured this out all by yourself, tested it, confirmed that it worked, and made it so we can totally escape through the library any time we want . . . and you're sitting here casually telling us about it like it's just some little idea you had?"

Henry bit his lip and nodded.

"You, my friend," Ava said, "are my hero."

Crow whooped in agreement, and they spent the entire rest of the afternoon thoroughly celebrating Henry's brilliant breakthrough.

Their next big step forward came when they decided to leave behind an Oath Scroll for Warden Pike. This was Ava's idea. She kept remembering the warden's face in the clock room, when he'd been so worried the Swickwit secret might not be safe that he'd become genuinely scary. He would probably be even angrier when he found out the three of them were gone, so they had to find some way to stop him from coming after them. They had a long way to travel to get to West Oz—at least three days of walking, according to the map they'd copied from a sofa-sized atlas in the library—and Ava didn't want to be looking over her shoulder the whole time, waiting for a furious Warden Pike to swoop down and drag them back to Swickwit.

So she buried herself in research for two entire afternoons, finally returning to the dorms with an Oath Scroll: a spell that would make any promise they wrote down impossible to break. She had written it carefully, laying out their promise to never tell the Swickwit secret to anyone who didn't already know. The scroll would make saying the words literally impossible from that day until the scroll was destroyed, and they were all very serious as they signed it and felt the oath take hold. It wasn't a pleasant feeling—the spell felt like a shower of pins and needles—but Ava thought they owed it to Warden Pike. He was only protecting his home, after all. She hoped it would be enough for him to let them go.

Two other interesting things happened that week.

The first was when Ava came back from the library one evening to find Tinabella had redecorated her half of the room.

The difference was dramatic. Tinabella's walls were midnight black, her sheets dark purple, and her wardrobe a sort of galactic acid green. There were blue firefly lights strung around her bed, bunches of dried herbs dangling from the ceiling, and spiky magical symbols drawn across the floor.

"Whoa!" Ava said, stopping in the doorway. "You're really settling in, huh?"

Tinabella looked up from her desk, where she was carving runes into her pencil holder with a chunk of crystal. She shrugged. "Felt like time."

Ava dropped her books on her bed, standing back to take in the full witchy effect. "I like it," she said. "It's very you. My side looks all plain and boring now."

"Yeah, well, that sounds about right," said Tinabella.

Ava blinked. She kept forgetting the two of them were no longer friends.

Tinabella huffed a sigh and put down her crystal. "Sorry," she said, unexpectedly. "I didn't mean that. Do you, you know, want to fix your side up? I can show you the decorating charm I found."

"Oh." Ava blinked again. "No, thanks. I think I'm good."

"Suit yourself."

They returned to an awkward silence.

This quiet version of Tinabella was the hardest thing for Ava to get used to, seeing as her roommate had almost never stopped talking for their first month of school. She missed that. Or she missed the fun and solidarity they used to share, anyway. It turned out it was hard to truly let a friendship go, but Ava was learning that sometimes that was your only choice. People changed fast, and you just had to let them.

Besides, Ava would be leaving in a few days, so long as the plan worked. Things wouldn't feel uncomfortable forever.

For now, she decided, opening a book and settling back against her pillow, she would keep to herself and enjoy the colorful new view. Tinabella might not be the nicest person Ava had ever met, but she really did have a great eye for design.

The other interesting thing that happened was Henry suddenly learning more magic. He was still scared all the time, but he paid attention in class, and on his third day he surprised everyone—including himself—by making his spell book float for almost ten whole seconds. The next day he turned a pencil into a pile of shavings. And the next he was the fourth person in the class to successfully create an illusion of a giant squirrel jumping out of the blackboard. He tried to hide it, but Ava could tell he was delighted at his sudden progress, and, judging by the way he kept mentioning his parents, relieved.

"I can't wait to get back and tell them," he said to Ava and Crow as they sprawled under their library table one afternoon. "Dean Waterwash can't expel me now. Only I don't even know how it's happening! Magic just makes sense here. Or maybe it's Professor Mulch; she's a really good teacher." He frowned. "I hope my parents aren't freaking out too much. I've only missed one letter, but I'm supposed to be writing to them every single week."

"Do your parents make a big deal out of things?" Ava asked.

Henry's eyes went as wide as they could go. "You have no idea."

The days flew by, and at last it was time. Their plans were memorized, they had food for the journey stashed in the library, and their packed bags were hidden in their closets.

They were set.

The dining hall served popcorn and waffles that night, and the three of them ate squeezed together on the broken love seat that had once been Ava and Tinabella's favorite dinner spot.

"Are you ready?" Ava asked the boys. She was feeling almost too nervous to eat, but the food was good, and she knew she'd need lots of energy for the long night ahead.

Crow calmly took a bite of the waffle-popcorn-maple-syrup sandwich he'd invented. "Oh, sure. It's gonna be awesome."

"I think so," said Henry. "At least, I'm looking forward to getting back."

"What's the dining hall like at WOW Academy?" Ava asked, realizing she had no idea.

Henry flinched as a big group of older students

transformed into lions, knocking over tables as they pounced on one another, roaring. "Not like this," he said.

Ava looked around at the sea of laughing, noisy kids. She could see why it made Henry nervous. The dining hall had grown more rambunctious with every passing week as everyone learned new magic. The teachers didn't seem to have any interest in calming things down, and there had been more than one all-school magical food fight lately. Who knew what dinner would be like by the end of the year?

To her surprise, Ava thought she might miss eating here. Just a bit.

They played card games in the Round Room after dinner, keeping an eye on the fresh slime they'd smeared across the library doorframe and filling up as much time as possible before they had to go to bed. When they finally did, Ava felt a stab of envy toward Henry and Crow. As roommates, they would be able to talk and run around and help keep each other awake. She would have to pretend to be asleep until Tinabella was snoring. Plus, if she actually did fall asleep, their plans would be ruined, since it was her job to sneak out and get the boys once the coast was clear on her end.

Ava didn't have long to wait before Tinabella returned,

smelling like woodsmoke and burnt snickerdoodles from whatever fun she'd been having with Carmelie and Dorian. She washed and changed, ignoring Ava, who was already under her covers to hide her clothes, then turned off her firefly lights and tumbled into bed.

"Good night," Ava whispered.

"Mm-mph," Tinabella replied.

Ava rolled over, staring into the dark, ready to keep herself awake for as long as it took.

A little flicker of sadness zigzagged across her heart. She had liked Tinabella once, liked her a lot. Just over a week ago they had been each other's only friends.

Ava would always remember their wild month together. She hoped Tinabella would be happy at Swickwit.

Goodbye, she thought, settling down for the long wait. *Good luck.*

21

THE ESCAPE

Tinabella took ages to fall asleep, so Ava kept herself awake by counting every worry she could think of for the journey ahead. Finally, the sound of steady breathing came from across the room, and she slipped out from under the covers, grabbed her bag, and eased her way into the hall.

Conjuring up a pea-sized light, she tapped softly on the boys' door. Crow answered with a bag over his shoulder and his usual calm smile on his face.

"Pretty outfit," he whispered.

"Thanks," said Ava, smiling back and smoothing down her cactus dress.

Crow joined her in the hall, followed by Henry, who had changed into his silver WOW Academy uniform.

"All set?" Ava breathed.

"All set," said Henry, looking nervous.

"Bye, room," Crow whispered. "You were a good home all these years, but it's time for me to go."

They tiptoed down the dormitory hall and into the soft lamplight of the Round Room.

"So far, so good!" said Crow.

"Wait!" Ava said. "What about the Oath Scroll we signed?"

"I left it on my desk," answered Henry. "With a note saying it's for Warden Pike."

Ava relaxed, for the moment.

They gathered around the library door, looking at one another anxiously. So far, only Henry had seen with his own eyes that this slime system actually worked. It was their first big moment of truth.

Ava reached out and gripped the door handle. She pushed . . .

The handle turned.

The library door opened with a creak.

Henry's wild plan had worked.

"What are you doing?" said a voice.

All three of them jumped like startled sand fleas, spinning around. There, standing between them and the dormitory door, was Tinabella.

"What—" Ava choked out. "How— Where— Why didn't we hear you?!"

Tinabella gave a satisfied smirk, pointing to her feet. "Found a footstep-silencing spell. I got tired of being noisy every time I wanted to be invisible."

Ava, Crow, and Henry stared at her in horror.

"Okayyy, so you want me to guess what you're up to," Tinabella said. "I obviously just caught you doing something bad, and you're carrying all those bags, so . . . I bet you're trying to escape from school again like you said."

"No!" said Ava.

"No!" said Henry.

"Totally!" said Crow.

Ava and Henry looked at him.

"Oh," said Crow. "Secret. Right. Sorry."

Tinabella snorted. "It's fine. I really don't care." She squinted past them at the open door. "That's something, though. How'd you get that open?"

"Don't tell her!" Henry hissed at Crow, who slapped both hands over his mouth.

But Ava recognized the glint in Tinabella's eye. Tinabella knew she could ruin their escape with one good scream any time she liked. They would have to answer her questions.

She gave a sigh and explained about the slime.

"Interesting," Tinabella said, crossing her arms. "Very interesting." She regarded them for a long moment, then glanced over her shoulder at the dorm hallway. "Tell you what, how about I help?"

The three friends blinked.

"Are you—are you saying you want to come with us?" Ava said.

"What? Ew, no!" Tinabella looked offended. "I'm saying I can clean the slime off this side of the door once you're gone, and the rest after class tomorrow. You know, because otherwise people might figure out how you got out? They're gonna be wondering when you don't show up for breakfast."

Ava was having trouble sorting out how she felt. "Okay, um, thanks," she said. "That would be great. But, you know, *why*?"

"Why am I helping?" Tinabella gave a theatrical shrug. "Maybe I'm an amazing friend. Maybe I'm the nicest person in the whole world. Or maybe I just want you three out of the way. I mean, with you gone, Ava, I finally get the whole room to myself."

Ava couldn't hold back a tiny smile, remembering her roommate's first attempt to get rid of her with a bucket of water.

"Besides," Tinabella went on, "I don't want any other kids finding out about this slime and portal business. It's a seriously powerful secret, and I am not sharing."

Ava looked at Crow. Crow looked at Henry. Henry looked at Ava.

"All right, then," she said. "We accept. Thanks."

After that, there was nothing left to do but leave. Crow gave Tinabella an enthusiastic handshake and stepped through into the library, Henry followed, and then only Ava was left, standing in the doorway with her ex–best friend.

Tinabella thrust out her chin. "So, you really did it? You found a way to get home?"

"I think so," said Ava. "If we're not here in the morning, then yes."

For one moment, a look of longing flashed over Tinabella's face. Then it vanished, and her glare returned. "Well, you never really did belong here anyway."

Ava stepped through the doorway, looking back. "I'll see if I can find a way to send you messages sometimes if you want. And, um, maybe go easy on the other kids? You and Carmelie are kind of a scary combination."

Tinabella gave an openly wicked grin. "Ha! No promises. I found out today Jadis is scared of paper clips. But sure, you could send me messages sometimes. If you want."

Ava smiled. With one last wave, she pulled the door shut behind her.

She let out a breath.

The first stage of their escape was over.

22

THE WAGON AGAIN

The escaping friends walked single file through the silent, shadowed library. Ava went in front, conjuring just enough light to weave a path through the tables and bookcases. Henry shivered in the middle. Crow hummed softly as he brought up the rear.

They had just retrieved the supplies they'd stashed under their meeting table when Crow gave a sharp hiss. Ava extinguished the light, and they stood frozen, hardly daring to breathe, as an enormous dark *something* floated past the shelves where they had been just a moment before.

It was shaped vaguely like a giant upright beetle, though there was a horrible humanness to its body and gait as it hobbled along through the air, sniffing and snuffling with quick, hoarse breaths. It stank of burning meat. In its six outstretched arms, it held a stack of crumbling, leather-bound books.

Ava fought down competing urges to run and hide under the table. She'd known leaving at night would be tricky, but in all her worrying she'd never considered what dangers might walk the halls of Swickwit after dark.

At last, the something passed them by, and after a long, watchful moment they started on their way again. Crow was no longer humming.

They encountered no other company as Ava led the boys along their twisting route, but after the third time having to backtrack and retrace their steps, she began to suspect the school was slowing them down, adding new turns and corridors and stretching the hallways out on purpose.

After a much longer journey than it should have been, they reached the secret stone door and stepped out of the walls of Swickwit.

The sky above the fog was patchy with clouds, with only a few faint stars peeking through. Henry and Crow relieved their nerves with whispered cheers and laughter, but Ava kept going, heading right for the Wicked Wagon. She didn't trust anything tonight. She wouldn't feel safe until they were on the other side of those glass hills— however that was going to happen.

The others hurried to follow, and at last the Wicked Wagon loomed up out of the fog.

"Wow," murmured Henry. "That is t-terrifying."

Crow ran a hand along the wagon's side. "I don't know.

It's smaller than I remember." He gave the ancient wood a pat. "It's kind of cute."

Ava had no idea how anyone could possibly call the Wicked Wagon *cute*, but it was their ticket across the boiling lake tonight, so she supposed she should think of it as a friend.

She pulled the bolt and eased the door open, wincing as the hinges screeched. The darkness inside was total.

Ava turned to the boys.

"In," she said, pointing.

Henry backed away, gazing in horror at the dark opening.

"N-no!" he yelped. "I can't go in there."

"You can if you want to get home."

"I'll go first," offered Crow. "Can I have a light?"

Ava conjured up an orb, and Crow ducked into the wagon, giving it another friendly pat on the way.

"Ooh," he said, crossing to sit on one of the benches. "There's lots of new graffiti!"

Reluctantly, Henry followed, and Ava came last, pulling the door closed behind her.

She looked around. The orb of light cast dense shadows in the boxy space, making random carvings punch out vividly:

Not my fault

Goodbye Platypus Lane

Dritten club forever!

I want to wake up

Ava remembered her first time in here, trapped and furious and afraid. It felt like years ago already.

She crossed to the window, looking out through the bars to the lake.

"Okay," she asked. "Everybody ready?"

"Ready!" said Crow and Henry together. Henry was clutching his bag, his eyes squeezed shut. Crow had his legs stretched out in front of him.

"Then here we go."

Ava took a deep breath, gathered her power, and reached out to the lake.

Focusing hard, she pulled the boiling water up the rocks, building it into a powerful wave. When it felt like enough, she scooped the wave forward, hoping to lift the wagon from underneath and carry it straight back into the water.

Instead, she hit a wall.

A foot from the Wicked Wagon, the water was being stopped by something she couldn't see. Ava gripped the bars and tried again.

"Is it working?" asked Henry, his eyes still squeezed shut.

"Not quite," Ava said. She was starting to feel a little

scared. If she failed at this, they were stuck, and it was way too early in their escape for that.

Crow joined her at the window. "Give it another go," he suggested.

Ava did, and once again the water met the invisible barrier. She tried sending the wave over the top of the wagon, but the barrier was everywhere, wrapped around them like some kind of dome. The boiling weight roared and splashed above their heads, but not a single drop could get through.

"Is it over?" Henry asked. "Are we across?"

With a grunt of frustration, Ava let her power go, feeling the water slide back into the lake, bubbling away as if nothing had happened.

"No," she said, kicking the nearest bench. "It didn't work."

"Oh." Henry opened his eyes. "Sorry."

"Probably gargoyle magic," Crow mused, plopping back down on his seat.

"Huh?" said Ava.

"Gargoyle magic. Professor Mulch did a lesson on it last year. They're really powerful. Gern must have cast a protection spell."

Ava stared at him. "And you didn't think that might be something you should tell us?"

Crow shrugged. "You seemed really certain this would work. Other people always know way more than I do."

"What do we do now?" asked Henry.

Both boys looked to Ava.

She gritted her teeth. If they couldn't use the Wicked Wagon as a boat, they would have to figure out some other way to get across the water.

She forced her tired, anxious brain to dig for more ideas, until finally she found one.

"Okay," she said. "We'll walk. The lake doesn't feel super deep. I'll clear a path right down to the bottom, and hopefully we can cross that way."

"Walk between the water?" Henry squeaked. "Are you sure you can hold it back until we reach the other side?"

Ava understood why Henry was scared. If she lost her hold on the boiling water for even a second, all three of them would be cooked alive.

"Yes," she said, deciding this was no time for self-doubt. "Yes, I can."

"Cool!" Crow jumped to his feet. "Let's go." He pushed open the wagon's door, then turned back. "Wait, won't the rocks or sand or whatever still be pretty hot? Like, hot enough to melt our shoes?"

Ava blinked. "Yes," she said. "That's smart thinking, Crow."

Crow's face lit up. "It is? Thanks!"

"It's also one more problem holding us back, and I'm seriously out of ideas. Unless anybody knows any foot-toughening spells?"

Crow shook his head sadly, but Henry sat up, a tentative smile sliding onto his face.

"I think," he said, "I can help."

23

THE BOILING LAKE

Ava, Henry, and Crow stood at the edge of the rocky slope, their bags and supplies bundled across their backs, staring down at the dark lake of boiling water.

"Are we certain this will work?" asked Crow.

"Not really," said Henry.

"But it's our only shot," noted Ava.

Crow nodded. "Cool. Which part happens first?"

Ava and Henry glanced at each other.

"Shoes first, I think?" said Ava. "That way I'm not standing here holding back the water."

Henry gulped.

"You've got this!" said Crow, patting him on the shoulder.

Henry squeezed his eyes shut and puffed out his cheeks, just like Ava had seen him do outside Dean Waterwash's office at West Oz Witch Academy. Last time he'd grown the soles of his shoes by a quarter of an inch. This time . . .

"Whoo-ooa!" Henry shouted, his eyes flying open as he zoomed upward.

"Hooray!" said Crow "You're taller than me now!"

And it was true. The soles of Henry's shoes were now three feet thick, and his pink-haired head was looking down at both his friends in shock.

"What happened?" asked Ava as Henry wobbled, finding his balance on his new stilts.

"I—I don't know. I did what I did before, only this time there was so much power. I barely even had to try."

"Looks like our buddy has leveled up!" said Crow.

Henry almost looked proud of himself.

"Are you gonna be okay up there?" Ava asked.

Henry held out his arms and took a few careful steps. "I think so? Maybe?"

"Well, I'd like my soles shorter than that if you can."

"I'll definitely try."

Henry closed his eyes and puffed out his cheeks, and a moment later Ava's shoes shot up several inches.

"I think I'm getting the hang of it," Henry said. He repeated the spell for Crow, who laughed as he bounced up.

"Nice going, Henry!" said Ava. "Guess it's my turn now."

Her stomach was in knots, but she refused to let nerves get the better of her. Her friends were about to trust her with their lives. She had to trust herself.

The tickling energy filled Ava as she reached out to the lake, and she pushed into it, lifting both arms to corral as much of the water as she could, focusing with all her might on exactly what she wanted. The lake bucked and heaved and churned—either fighting or playing, she couldn't tell—until, with a sucking *shwoomp,* the boiling waters parted into two towering waves, exposing a narrow path of bone-white sand leading directly to the other side.

Cautiously, Ava let her arms drop, holding on with nothing but her mind. The walls held.

Henry and Crow cheered.

"I think I should go first since I'm shortest now," said Ava. "Then Crow, then Henry? So we can all see?"

The others nodded.

Ava wasn't sure taking deep breaths was helping anymore, but she took one anyway, then led the way down the slope and onto the sand.

Her shoes sizzled.

"Okay, soles definitely melting!" she said. "Can you do that spell again while we walk, Henry?"

"I think so. Just shout when you need it."

"Awesome. What should we shout?"

"HOT FEET!" shouted Crow.

Henry smiled. "That works."

"Good," said Ava. "Let's get this over with."

And they set out.

The walk was even harder than Ava had expected.

The tall shoes were wobbly no matter how careful she was, and it was difficult to concentrate on both the water and keeping her footing. The air around them was scorching hot and smelled unpleasantly of iron, melting rubber, and, for some reason, pickles. She kept her eyes on the sand, not letting herself think about tripping and crashing into the water, or losing her hold on her power, or any of the other ways this incredibly dangerous journey could go wrong.

She was getting ready to call her second "Hot feet!" when she heard Crow and Henry crunch to an abrupt stop, then gasp. She stopped, too, looking around, and choked back a scream.

Something huge was sliding through the water beside them. Something huge and black and scaly, just under the surface of the right-hand wall.

Sweat stung Ava's eyes, but she didn't dare raise an arm to wipe it away as the creature coiled in on itself, revealing razor-sharp fins along its back. For one terrible moment a face stared out from the bubbling darkness. A face bigger than the three of them put together. A face made of teeth, and more teeth, and two bottomless, shining eyes.

The tip of a whip-thin tail pierced the wall, scattering boiling droplets at their feet.

Then, in a twisting flicker of scales, the creature vanished into the lake.

All three of them stood there, motionless, too transfixed to move, until Ava let out a yelp.

"Ouch! Hot feet!"

The spell broke, and Henry puffed out his cheeks, boosting her back above the sand.

"That," murmured Crow, shaking his head, "was incredible!"

"And I thought you were silly for thinking there might be fish in here," Henry said weakly.

"That was no fish," said Ava.

They stared at the wall in silence for another moment, then started off again.

Ava kept one eye fixed on the water after that, but whatever they'd seen didn't reappear. As she walked, she wondered what kind of creature could live in boiling water, and what it ate, and why she hadn't known it was there when she was holding so much of the lake in her power. Finally, she decided there were some things better left well enough alone.

At long last the path ended, and Ava climbed up onto a narrow strip of rock between the boiling lake and the hills. Crow followed a moment later, but Henry stopped, standing all alone on the last bit of sand.

"Sorry," he called. "My shoes are still too tall, and I can't do the spell in reverse. I just need to melt them down a bit more."

Ava and Crow watched, fighting smiles, while Henry slowly shrank. When he was back to his regular height, he scrambled up onto the rocks beside them, and Ava let go of her magic. She sighed with relief as the water splashed back into place, feeling a deep glow of pride under her tiredness.

She had done it. She had held on through worry, fear, and danger. She had gotten her friends across the boiling lake.

She was ready to face the hills of broken glass.

24

CROW'S SECRET

The hills of broken glass were beautiful up close, shimmering like the dome of WOW Academy under the stars. But Ava knew that beauty was a lie. Every gleaming surface was an edge waiting to cut. Every sparkle was a point ready to pierce.

Just the idea of climbing the hills made her mind flinch away. She couldn't bear the thought of putting her foot on that slope, hearing the crunch and snap as she gave it her weight. She could feel the imagined sound in her teeth.

It was almost enough to make her wish she were safe in her bed in Nettle Tower. For a moment, Ava pictured her classmates, asleep and dreaming up and down the dormitory hall. She pictured the quiet, empty desks of the root-wrapped classroom and the clamor of the Round Room at breakfast. Swickwit, for all its messy confusion, had become . . . familiar, and a strange weight touched her heart as she turned to look back over the lake.

"Ready for this?" Henry asked, stepping up beside her.

Ava shook herself. "I guess," she said. "I just wish I knew what was coming."

They looked to Crow, who was taking off his bags. "Can you two carry these?" he asked. "I can't do it if I'm wearing them."

Their curiosity growing, Ava and Henry looped Crow's bags over their shoulders.

Crow gave the hills a worried glance, then took a deep breath, letting it out slowly. "I've seen you doing that," he said to Ava. "I hope it helps."

"Me too. Are you certain you can do . . . whatever it is?"

Crow nodded. "I know I can. I just want to make sure I keep you two safe. And also . . ." He paused, rubbing the back of his head. "Please don't judge me."

"We won't," whispered Henry.

Crow was beginning to scare Ava. What was he going to do? What was this one mysterious talent he possessed? What was so strange or dangerous that he'd let himself flunk Nettle twice and stopped himself from learning any other magic at all rather than reveal it?

Rocks crunched as Crow shifted his feet. "Don't move," he said. "And try not to scream."

At first, there was nothing. Ava heard Crow whispering, the sound dancing in and out of the constant bubbling of the lake.

Then the hair on the back of her neck stood up. Tension shimmered through the air like a pulse just on the edge of hearing.

Before them, Crow began to . . . glow.

It was faint at first, just a gleam outlining his legs and arms. Then it grew, intensifying, speeding up, until, with a *whomp* that made Ava's ears pop, Crow's skeleton caught fire.

That was the only way she could make sense of it. Crow stood before them, blazing a fierce, burning red from the inside out. Every one of his bones, skull to ribs to toes, was perfectly visible, as if the rest of him was just a thin scrap of paper wrapped around a lamp. The red glow reflected off the fog. The air throbbed with power. Ava heard Henry whimper.

Crow raised his arms, and the light grew stronger, then stronger again. The pressure built until Ava thought something had to give, that either she and Henry were going to catch fire, too, or the whole world was going to end. Then Crow snapped his wrists together, hands just above his heart, and pushed his palms out, hard, toward the broken glass.

An enormous fiery sphere burst from him, searing its way directly into the hill. Ava could see it burrowing on and on, the light scattering through the glass as it went, until somewhere far ahead it finally slowed, and faded, and died.

Where it had gone in, there was now a tunnel of melted glass.

Crow, looking normal again, slumped over, bracing his hands on his knees. There was a faint tinkling somewhere high above, then silence.

"Whew!" Crow said. "It's been a while since I did that."

Ava conjured a small light. Crow looked over at them.

"So yeah," he said. "That's my magic."

"Wow," breathed Ava.

"What is it?" murmured Henry.

Crow straightened up, stretching his shoulders. "I didn't know for the longest time. I just woke up one day and I could do it. I found out pretty fast it was dangerous. I— People got hurt. People who were taking care of me. I refused to show anyone after that, so I couldn't find out more. But I finally tracked it down in a book in the Swickwit library. It's called Bone Fire, and, well"—he looked away—"it's supposed to be one of the most wicked kinds of magic there is. Almost no one can do it. Most people who could turned really, really evil."

Ava's heart twinged. She felt like she suddenly understood Crow a lot more.

"Well, you're not evil," she said. "But I've never seen

anything like that. I get why you didn't want to show it in class. But you're probably the most powerful kid at Swickwit."

Crow scuffed at the ground, looking embarrassed. "Maybe," he said. "I guess. In this one thing. Only it's never been, you know, useful before."

They all turned to look at the glass tunnel.

"Is it safe?" asked Henry.

"Should be." Crow stepped forward to examine the entrance, and Ava sent another light to help him see. "I think we'll be okay," he said. "So long as we don't touch the walls."

Ava swallowed hard at the idea of walking into that fragile tunnel beneath actual tons of broken glass. It would require a real leap of faith in Crow. There wasn't any choice, though, and the others had trusted her with their lives crossing the lake. She could be brave like them.

"Guess we'd better go," she said, putting as much confidence as she could into her voice. "The night's passing."

Crow went first, bending over a little to fit. The tunnel was slightly shorter than him, but wide enough for them to not have to worry about their packs and bags. Henry went next, and Ava took up the rear, sending her lights ahead and behind. Their glow illuminated walls of melted glass so sleek and full of rainbows she had to restrain herself from running a hand down them. The ground beneath their feet was melted glass, too, rippled and smooth.

"Watch every step," said Crow from the front, his voice echoing strangely. "And remember about not touching the walls."

Ava and Henry nodded, and they set out.

They went slowly at first, wide-eyed and cautious, but soon settled into a steady rhythm. The air was warm and smelled of hot glass and lightning, and the tunnel carved forward in a straight, unwavering line, making the constantly changing fractals of the rainbow walls the only sure sign they were even moving.

After ten minutes they came to a dead end, and Crow explained he would have to repeat the Bone Fire spell. Ava and Henry hung back while Crow gathered and released his terrifying power again, and they continued on.

Ava almost succeeded in not thinking about how much sharp glass was pressing down over her head. Almost. Every time it came scraping at her mind, she forced herself to think about waffles, or to try to come up with a name for the creature they'd seen in the lake, or to imagine how wonderful it was going to be to talk to her family and Peaches again.

Crow repeated his spell twice more, using less power

each time, until, at last, they felt a delicious coil of cool night air rushing along the tunnel to meet them.

They hurried for the exit. Ava was so excited she stumbled, only just catching herself from crashing into the wall as the boys vanished ahead of her.

"Phew!" she said, stepping back into the welcoming night. "Thank goodness!"

The glass hills rose huge and silent behind them. Ahead, rolling grass stretched on and on, marked here and there with trees. The sky had cleared completely, and a perfect crescent moon was rising among the stars to the south. There was no sign of people, or houses, or roads. They were quite alone.

They were safe.

Ava breathed in lungfuls of fresh air, filling to the brim with happiness as the reality of what they'd just done sank in.

"Guys!" she said, turning to her friends. "We did it! We actually did it! We escaped!"

Crow threw back his head and whooped. Ava stretched her arms overhead and spun in a giddy circle. Henry did a self-conscious little jig.

"Can we do anything about the tunnel?" Ava asked after they'd settled down. "We don't want anyone from the school seeing it."

"No problem." Crow dug a small rock out of the grass, took careful aim at the dark entrance, and threw.

The rock hit the tunnel wall with a *plink*.

A faint crackling reached their ears, like someone stepping on a dried leaf.

There was a moment of silence.

Then the tunnel collapsed in a storm of shattering glass, the whole hill shifting as it crushed the fragile pathway to dust all the way back to the lake.

They listened, wide-eyed and frozen, until the last of the splintering glass had settled.

"Wow," said Henry. "I'm, um, super glad I didn't know the tunnel was that fragile."

"Me too," said Ava.

She turned away from the hills and looked up at the sky.

"That's west over there," she said, pointing across the grass to a triangle of blue-white stars. The Dragon's Tooth, they called it in the desert. "I know we could use a break, but we really should keep going. We don't want to be anywhere near school when morning comes."

Crow took back his bags, opening them to hand out snacks and water. When everyone was ready, they shouldered their gear and started the next stage of their journey.

Ava was tired, but she didn't think she'd ever felt so happy.

They had really done it. They were free. She and her friends had left the School for Wicked Witches behind. For good.

25

WALKING AND WONDERING

Ava had never seen so much grass before. It rolled away in all directions, dark under the moon and starlight. Off to their right, a shining clump of green glowed against the horizon.

"What's that?" asked Ava, pointing to it as they walked along.

Henry and Crow looked over, then raised their eyebrows at Ava.

"That's the Emerald City," said Henry.

"You know, the capital of Oz?" said Crow. "Where the Wizard lived?"

"Oh," Ava said. "I think maybe I heard of it once. It looks pretty."

Henry shook his head in disbelief.

"Life must be pretty different out there in the desert," Crow said.

Ava shrugged. "I guess it is kind of far from the big cities and everything. But it's home." She swallowed a lump in her throat.

They walked and walked and walked. Finally, they

reached an old gazebo on a little hill. The roof was half gone, but the floor was sturdy and clean, so they settled in for a rest.

The crescent moon was flying high above them now, peeking in through the gaps in the roof. Crow got out more snacks, yawning hugely.

"Same he-ee-re!" said Ava, joining him. "I wonder what time it is."

"Feels really late," Henry said, peeling a plorange. "It's eerie being the only ones up."

"Kind of fun, though," said Crow, around a mouthful of honeycomb sandwich.

Ava unrolled their map from her pack and conjured a light. "Okay, so this gazebo isn't marked, but since we haven't reached this big river yet, I'd say we're about . . . here."

"And where's your school?" asked Crow.

Ava placed a finger on the map.

"Um, Ava?" Henry said.

"What?" She looked to where her finger was pointing: a dark blotch at the center of Oz.

Swickwit.

"Whoa!" she yelped, trying to cover her horror with a laugh. "Haha! Don't know why I did that!"

Her face hot and her mind reeling—*what had she been*

thinking?!—she stabbed her finger firmly onto the left side of the map, almost poking a hole through WOW Academy.

Henry shot Ava a curious look, but Crow whistled, walking the distance with his fingers. "That's a long way. And there's the Dark Forest and all these hills and valleys to get past."

"Yup!" said Ava, deciding to pretend absolutely nothing strange had just happened. "But there's a big road coming up called the Yeeber that will bring us close to WOW Academy. It shouldn't be *too* rough."

"My feet hurt already," Henry said. "I didn't really think about how much walking this would be."

"Same," said Ava. "Let's take a solid break here, then do one more push before we stop to sleep."

The boys nodded, and they all settled into a comfortable silence, eating and stargazing and trading yawns.

"I still can't believe we really did it," Ava said, after a while. "I mean, I obviously hoped we would. But, you know, wow."

"*I* can't believe Crow's magic," said Henry. "Talk about *power*."

They looked over at Crow, who was staring at his shoes.

"What's up?" asked Ava.

Crow opened and shut his mouth a few times. "No one at Swickwit knows I can do Bone Fire," he said finally. "Partly 'cause it's way too dangerous to do at school. But mostly because I wanted to keep it a secret." He was speaking slowly, letting each thought settle before he let it out. "I know I'm not the smartest kid around. And I'm not cool or anything. But I hope people think I'm nice. I try to be nice because I know how it feels when people aren't. And if people found out I can do Bone Fire, they might think I'm evil or, you know, sneaky and powerful instead. And I'm not. I'm just a kid who wants to make some friends and get through school. I don't want everyone who sees me to think, 'Oh, it's Bone Fire Guy.' I don't want to be Bone Fire Guy. You know?"

Ava's heart gave a squeeze as she nodded. Crow really was a good person.

Even so, a new worry was elbowing its way forward like Carmelie in the dinner line: What if WOW Academy wouldn't let Crow in? If Bone Fire had this horrible reputation, and it was the only thing Crow could do, then what would happen when they made him demonstrate his magic? He would probably get kicked out if he refused, but if he showed them, chances were Dean Waterwash would bundle him back to Swickwit faster than blinking. It would be awful to travel all that way together only to say goodbye.

"At least you know what your power is, Crow," said Henry. "You'll probably be amazing with all sorts of fire spells someday. And Ava's got her water talent. I don't have anything like that. I'm not smart or cool, either. I'm just scared all the time." He picked at a splinter in the gazebo floor. "There's nowhere I fit in."

Ava's heart squeezed all over again hearing Henry talk like that.

"Well, when we're classmates at WOW Academy, we can work on fitting in together," she said briskly, squashing down her worries and deciding to deal with them later. "Oh, and for what it's worth, I think both of you are totally cool."

Eventually, they agreed to get moving again, and everyone groaned as they stood up, wincing over their sore feet.

"I wish, wish, wish we could find a way to get there faster," said Henry.

"I wish we could fly," said Crow.

"Come on," Ava said. "Let's get in a few more miles."

They walked on, steering west by the stars. This deep into the night, Oz revealed a strange, unsettled side of itself. Sickly yellow lights danced in circles across distant fields. A half-collapsed cave they stumbled across echoed with a constant, sorrowful moan. Tiny creatures darted through the grass around them, always just out of view as they hunted one another with fierce, chittering cries.

Once, a flock of dark birds flew low overhead, their wings blotting out the stars and their thin calls filling the travelers with a kind of dizzy chill. A single long feather drifted down as they passed, settling at Ava's feet. It was beautiful, bright gold on top, jet-black beneath, and Ava's fingers were just about to close on it for a souvenir when she noticed it had burned all the grass around it to a crisp. She snatched her fingers back, and they resumed walking, keeping one eye on the sky.

Crow spotted the road first.

"Look!" he said as they came panting over the top of a steep hill. "Look, look, look!"

Ava and Henry looked. A rushing river was cutting right across their path. A sturdy bridge led across it, and on the other side a wide brick road coming down from the northeast made a turn, carving out due west.

"Yes!" said Ava. "That's the bridge we were aiming for. That road must be the Yeeber." She pumped a tired fist in the air. "Go team!"

The three friends stumbled down the hill, over the bridge, and onto the waiting path.

"Okay, so we found it," said Henry. "Can we please go

to sleep now? Look, there are trees right there where we can camp."

"Sounds good to me," said Crow. "Ava?"

But Ava wasn't listening. From the moment they'd set foot on the road, her sense of magic had been going absolutely haywire. Dropping to her knees, she conjured a light and prodded the surface they were standing on.

"Um, Ava?" called Henry. "Why are you staring at the road like that?"

"And—whoa, why are you laughing?" added Crow.

"The bricks!" Ava wheezed. "The road! It's yellow!"

Henry and Crow looked at each other.

"Yeah . . ." said Henry. "This is the Yellow Brick Road? It's famous?"

"Some people call it the YBR."

Ava dissolved back into laughter. "Saw that on the map," she finally managed. "I thought it was pronounced Yeeber!"

"Oh, funny," said Henry.

"But they're yellow!" Ava repeated, wiping her eyes. "Do you know what else is yellow? West Oz brick moss!"

The boys stared at her.

"This entire road is made of brick moss—and that means some of it was definitely grown by *my family*!"

"Hey, that's cool!" said Crow. "The YBR is the most important road in Oz."

"It's really neat," said Henry. "But why are you so excited, exactly?"

"Because this changes *everything*."

Ava jumped to her feet, buzzing. Brick moss was where her magic had started. She knew it inside and out. And she had some schooling under her belt now.

She planted her hands on her hips, suddenly wide awake and ridiculously happy. "Forget sleeping, guys," she announced, "and forget three days of walking. I think I can get us to West Oz Witch Academy by breakfast."

26

THE YELLOW BRICK ROAD

"Everybody ready?" Ava asked.

"Let's do it!" called Crow.

"Are you sure this is safe?" Henry mumbled.

They were sitting in a row on the Yellow Brick Road. Ava was in front, holding on to Henry's outstretched feet. Henry sat behind her, holding on to Crow's. Crow was in back, holding on to Henry.

"Of course I'm not sure," Ava said. "I've never done this before."

Henry made a wheezy sort of noise.

"Oh, stop it." Ava gave his feet a shake. "It'll be fine. The worst that can happen is it doesn't work, and then we'll just set up camp and go to sleep. Now everybody quiet so I can concentrate!"

The others settled, but Ava swallowed hard. The truth was, she had no idea what might be about to happen. She was proud of her daring idea and definitely hoped it would work, but her confidence was mostly an act. There was every chance this could go pretty seriously wrong.

Crossing her fingers, Ava sank into her power and reached out for the river beside them.

She gasped as she made contact. It was *nothing* like connecting with the boiling lake. This water was fierce and constantly on the move, and it absolutely did not care about her. It shrugged off her attempts to shape it again and again, refusing to be controlled.

Ava was a little surprised at how angry that made her. The river was blocking her great idea! She clenched her jaw and dug in deep, flexing her power in a stern, uncompromising way she'd never attempted before. Flashes of memories flickered through her mind: Jadis gleefully smashing statues; Dean Waterwash forcing her into the Wicked Wagon; the WOW Academy great hall right before her monstrous juicy-pop tree explosion.

Beside them, the river kicked and bucked, splashing up onto the bank. Henry screamed.

"No! Wait!" Ava gritted her teeth. "I. Have. Got. This!"

For one awful moment, she really, really didn't. The river was pushing back, overwhelming her connection to her power, battering her magic into chaos. Ava felt hot tears forming behind her eyes, and it was her stubborn refusal to cry that finally did it.

A tiny gap appeared in the river's strength, and she

twisted into it, gasping as she wrenched an enormous ball of water up and out and into the air.

"Yes!" called Crow. "Nice one!"

Trembling slightly, Ava floated the captive sphere over to her. The water swirled and spun, wanting to keep moving, to hurry onward like the river it had come from, to cover ground.

Good thing that's what I want, too, thought Ava.

She lowered the globe onto the road between her feet and shifted focus, encouraging the dried moss to soak it up. In moments the bricks had become full and bloated, pushing against one another until the roadway bulged like a balloon.

"Is it working?" Henry asked, watching over her shoulder.

Ava shushed him and gave the water a final tug, dragging it back under the three of them in one quick burst.

"Ooh!" Henry yelped as they all bounced up.

"That's cold!" said Crow. "And whoa, hey, is this going to damage the YBR?"

Ava eyed the road in front of her. The freshly drained bricks were in disarray, squidging out to the sides with big gaps in between. It looked like the answer to Crow's question was probably *yes*.

But, okay, what did that mean? Did it mean Ava should

give up on her brilliant idea? Miss out on the chance to cut their three-day journey down to one night? That was an awful lot to lose for the sake of a few bricks.

Besides, Ava's own family had made some of these bricks—maybe even most—so shouldn't she be allowed to use them in her hour of need? Bricks were replaceable, and saving herself and two other kids from the dangers of walking halfway across Oz had to be more important. Right?

"It'll be fine," she said, making her decision. "The moss should go back to how it was after a bit."

"Really?" asked Henry.

"Trust me." Ava pushed down the uncomfortable feelings at the back of her mind. "If there's one thing I know, it's brick moss. The road will be fine."

It wasn't a lie, exactly. For all she knew, the road *would* heal itself. And if it didn't, well, maybe that would mean more orders for bricks, and more money for her family, and what was wrong with that? The road would be back to normal *eventually*, one way or another.

"So, we're good," Ava said, making a few final adjustments. "Hold on tight, you two. Deep breaths. And off . . . we . . . go!"

Ava knew if she stopped to think about exactly how she was doing it, they would crash. So she did her best not to think at all as she kept the rolling bulge of water racing along with the three of them balanced precariously on top.

The wind whuffled in their ears, and Ava's nose would not stop running, and their bottom halves were soaked and freezing, but none of that really mattered. They were moving faster than any of them ever had gone in their lives. Faster than the train from Muzzlewump. Faster than the Wicked Wagon. Faster than a dream.

There was one thought Ava couldn't completely block out, though: the worrying scale of her power. Before she'd even learned to use it, her water magic had destroyed the great hall and gardens of West Oz Witch Academy. A few weeks of lessons later and she'd gained enough control to hold back a boiling lake, steal part of a raging river, and lead her friends on a nighttime joyride across Oz, wrecking a major road in the process.

If she was honest, the whole thing scared her just a little. It was a giddy feeling having this much magic, and she loved every chance she got to let it loose, but underneath the rush Ava didn't always feel comfortable. Could anything good come this easily? Wasn't there something, well, *wicked* about having so much power without doing anything to earn it?

Crow let out a happy laugh behind her, reveling in

their speed as they zoomed up another hill, and Ava remembered what he'd told them about Bone Fire. That was a dangerous power, too, but Crow had kept it under control, accepting years of serious social consequences rather than put anyone else at risk.

Ava felt uncomfortable all over again as she realized that if their powers had been reversed, she couldn't promise herself she would have done the same.

Time slipped into a hazy in-between as they pushed on and on and on. Ava kept her eyes ahead, watching out for other travelers, but thankfully the road stayed clear.

Not that they were alone under the stars. Oz by night continued to surprise them, revealing its mysteries in flashes on either side.

They passed an ancient tiptoeing tortoise, its lacquered shell barely visible beneath a tower of broken teapots.

Cold light glowed from the windows of three ramshackle huts stalking on chicken feet through a grove of plorange trees.

A lightning storm raged endlessly inside a ring of standing stones.

The Dark Forest swallowed them as they sped along, harsh growls and glowing eyes racing alongside the shivering young witches for ten spine-chilling minutes until all at once they were through, and the forest became just one more obstacle melting away into a dream behind them.

After a few hours, Ava became aware of a change in the darkness around them. She risked a glance back and saw the faint yellow-white glow of dawn nudging the eastern horizon.

She also got her first look at the boys' faces since they'd started their wild ride. Crow appeared tired but cheerful. Henry looked like he was back in the clock room with the wolf.

"How are you holding up?" she called over the wind. "I think we're not too far now. Maybe just another hour or—"

"Watch out!" yelled Crow and Henry, pointing.

Ava turned and gasped.

They were coming over the crest of a hill, and the landscape before them opened up into a broad plain. Across the plain Ava saw the gleaming towers of a city framed between mountains behind and farms and fields in front.

And at the bottom of the hill, sprawling right across the Yellow Brick Road ahead of them, was a circus.

27

THE CIRCUS

"Aaaah!" screamed Ava as they rocketed toward the tangle of tents.

The red-and-black stripes of the big top loomed directly across their path, and if she didn't do something quick, they were going to smash right into it.

Ava abandoned her hold on the water and, to her enormous relief, they immediately began to slow as the spinning sphere beneath them drained away to nothing.

Shaking, shivering, and very, very wet, the three friends slid to a squelching stop just outside the big-top entrance.

They all groaned as they got to their feet.

"Never again," Henry said, hugging himself.

"Aw, it wasn't so bad." Crow stretched his arms over his head. "Going fast felt amazing! That was seriously brilliant, Ava."

"Thanks!" Ava entirely agreed with Crow's assessment, especially after her struggle with the river. "But we're not done yet."

She glared at the enormous silk tent blocking their

way. What inconsiderate person would set up a circus right in the middle of a popular road? It had totally ruined their chances of getting to WOW Academy by breakfast.

"Hey, Ava?" Crow said. "Didn't you say you could dry us off?"

"Huh?" Ava turned to see both boys shivering. "Oh! Yes, sorry! Here." She sent a ripple of power over them all, pulling the water out of their clothes and releasing it into the soil.

"We aren't, um, going in there, are we?" asked Henry as the boys joined her at the entrance to the big top.

Ava nodded. "I think we have to. Did you see how far the circus went? We'd have to walk all the way around it to get back to the road."

"I like circuses," said Crow. "They have plorange cotton candy."

"I'm not sure this one does." Henry shivered again. "Can't you feel it? There's something . . . wicked about this place."

Ava knew what Henry meant. There was an edge to the air, an alert, watchful sort of tension, like the whole circus was alive. Alive and listening.

On the other hand, there didn't seem to be any alternatives. The only way past the circus was through.

She looked behind them again, where the first

fingers of the approaching dawn were pushing pink and golden above the hill.

"We'd better get this over with," she said. "People might be waking up soon."

Adjusting her bags across her shoulders, Ava pushed the tent flap open and stepped into the darkness. Henry and Crow followed.

They stood close together as their eyes adjusted. The dim red light filtering in through the silk made the huge space feel like the inside of an oven, and there was a complicated smell in the air, like hay, peanuts, and hot metal.

The Yellow Brick Road carried on before them, running clear and empty to the other end of the big top. To either side, the ground was hidden beneath booths and stalls advertising food, fortune-telling, games, and souvenirs. Stages rose around the tent's edges, their signs showcasing feats of daring and muscle and magic, while scores of flags hung like bats from the far-off ceiling, every one displaying a pair of ivory fangs dripping blood.

There was no one in sight, human or animal, but Ava, linking arms with Henry and Crow, still felt certain they were not alone.

The circus remained eerily still as they tiptoed forward, but as they reached the very center of the big top, a snuffling growl broke the quiet.

The three friends froze.

"Where did that come from?" Ava breathed.

"Over there, I think," whispered Crow, pointing to a platform behind a candleberry pie stand, where the top of a large cage was visible.

Henry coughed nervously. "Should— Should we go look?"

"Maybe?" Ava said. "This place is super creepy, but I kind of want to know what that was."

"Let's do it," said Crow. "We're always going to wonder, otherwise."

They left the road, Henry staying carefully in between the others, and wove their way through the carts and stalls.

All of them gasped as the source of the growling came into view.

The cage atop the platform was enormous, almost the size of the Round Room back at Nettle Tower. The bars were made of gleaming iron. And there, lying fast asleep in the center of it all, a chain around his neck, was Gern the gargoyle.

28

THE BARGAIN

"Gern!" Ava yelped, forgetting to whisper.

Henry shushed her, but it was too late. The dark blue gargoyle stirred, stretched, and opened his stone eyes.

"'Allo!" he rumbled, blinking. The chains around his neck and wings rattled as he sat up and settled back onto his wolf haunches. He wore the same stone shirt, vest, flat cap, and suspenders as the last time Ava had seen him. "Wot's this about? Show's not till this evenin'."

He peered closer at them.

"'Old on. I know you." He nodded at Ava and Crow. "You two are wicked 'uns! An' you"—he nodded at Henry—"yer . . . 'oo are you?"

"I'm H-Henry," Henry said. "Henry B-Buffle."

"Nice t' meet yeh, Henry Buffle. I'm Gern. I like yer pink 'air."

"Gern!" Ava interrupted. "What is going on? Why are you in that cage?!"

The gargoyle shrugged. "Got captured, didn't I?" He frowned. "Why are *you* out o' school? That's s'posed to be impossible."

"Well, we did it anyway," Ava said. "We're going back to West Oz Witch Academy."

"Soun's like a good story there! An' what, yeh thought ye'd stop fer a quick visit to the circus on the way?"

"We didn't mean to come to the circus," said Crow. "It was blocking the road."

"Do you need help?" asked Henry, who seemed to be getting accustomed to Gern's terrifying appearance. "Do you want us to r-rescue you?"

"That'd be grand!" The gargoyle gave Henry a wink. "But I don't know how ye'd go about it."

"Well, we *are* witches," said Ava. "And what's the point of that if we can't rescue a friend?" She turned to the others. "Come on, huddle up."

But after several minutes of whispered discussion, Ava had to admit they were no closer to a solution.

"Sorry," she said, turning back to Gern. "We do have powers, but none of them are the right sort. I mean, Crow here could definitely break this cage open . . ."

"But not without breaking you open, too," finished Crow. Gern whistled.

"Ugh!" said Ava. "This is awful. We can't just leave you here!" She reached out both hands and had only a moment to spot the alarm on Gern's face before her fingers wrapped around the bars.

With a whoosh, a swoosh, and a flash of metal, she found herself inside the cage beside him.

"Hey!" said Crow, leaping forward.

"Ava!" said Henry, doing the same.

"No!" Ava cried, but it was too late. Crow tried to stop, Henry bumped into him, and with another whoosh, swoosh, and flash, all four of them were trapped in the cage together.

At once, a deep, echoing laughter filled the tent, coming from everywhere and nowhere. The flags and banners began rippling in a wind none of them could feel.

"Oh no," whispered Gern. "She's comin'! Right, wha'ever ye do, don't tell her yer from Swickwit!"

"Don't tell who?" asked Crow.

"H-her," said Henry, pointing.

Across the sprawling circus, a woman had appeared, floating in the middle of the air.

She could have been twenty or a hundred and twenty—there was no way to tell under the jewels and makeup and cascade of black, glossy feathers she had instead of hair. Her skin was pale lilac, smooth as glass. She wore an elaborate green silk gown with enormous shoulder pads set with spikes. Her hands glittered with rings. Her eyes sparkled like cold fire. Her teeth as she smiled were red.

She was, clearly, a witch. And seeing as they were all

locked inside a cage and she was laughing outside it, Ava was pretty sure she was a wicked one.

The woman floated over and came to rest on the platform.

"And what have we here?" she cooed in a high, sweet voice that made Ava's hair stand on end. She dragged a finger across the bars, examining the three kids. "Whoooo are youuuu?"

Ava gulped. "Us? We're just, uh, travelers!"

"Kid travelers!" said Henry.

"Out traveling," added Crow. "Like kids do."

One eyebrow arched on the beautiful face.

"Really? Is that truuuuue?"

"Yes!" Ava tried to sound confident. "And who are youuu? I mean *you*?"

"Me?" The woman touched a hand to her collarbone, just above a superb necklace shaped like a snake with a rainbow of square jewels running down its back. Ava noticed a gap where one color was missing. She peered closer, and a memory prickled at the back of her mind. Something she'd seen before.

"I," the woman continued, "am Vivienne Morderay. The *great* Vivienne Morderay. The *feared* Vivienne Morderay. The *adored* Vivienne Morderay. Vivienne Morderay, the most powerful sorceress of them all."

Ava felt her blood go cold. She had heard of the wicked Vivienne Morderay all the way out in the desert. Dean Waterwash had even compared Ava to her while lecturing her in her office. If the stories were true, Vivienne Morderay had been crisscrossing Oz for nearly a century, moving from disguise to disguise, gathering riches and power and ruining lives wherever she went.

"Nice to meet you," said Crow, waving.

Vivienne Morderay narrowed her eyes at him.

"What," she said, "dooo youuu three want? Why did youuu try to free my gargly-goyle?"

"Your what?" said Ava.

"My gargly-goyle! He is mine. I caught him. And he will work for me in my circus until he has paid back his debt. Youuuu see, children, long ago this gargly-goyle stole something very precious from me."

"I never did!" For the first time, Gern sounded upset. "I keep tellin' ye, gargoyles don't steal! Yeh must've mislaid wha'ever you lost!"

Vivienne Morderay waved a finger, and an iron band appeared around Gern's mouth, locking it shut.

"Wh-what did he steal?" Henry asked.

"Something precious beyond measure. Powerful beyond your wildest dreams. More radiant than ten thousand suns shining upon a galaxy of diamond-encrusted stars."

They stared blankly at her.

"Jewelry," she said. "It was jewelry. And this beast stole it from me on my way tooo schoool! Me, an innocent child with barely one wicked deed tooo my name!"

Ava fought down a gasp. She had to be talking about Swickwit and the Wicked Wagon. Why else would Gern be involved?

"Sounds rough," said Crow. "Will you let us out now, please?"

Vivienne Morderay smiled a very nasty smile and shook her head. "Oh no-no-no-no-no. Youuu children tried to steal from me tooo. Tried to take my gargly-goyle. It's circus work for youuu until I feel justice has been served."

"How long will that take?" Ava asked.

"Oh, not long." Their captor was almost purring. "Forty years. Or perhaps thirty. It will depend on how hard youuu work."

Henry started crying. Crow started arguing. Gern made angry noises behind his gag.

Ava grabbed the bars. "You can't do this!" she yelled. "We're witches, too! We'll break out, and then you'll be sorry!"

Vivienne Morderay laughed. "Oh, little witches are youuu? Good little witches? Well, my sweet, youuu should know that this cage does more than keep youuu in. It also blocks your magic. Gargly-goyles are quite magical, after all. I suppose I'll just have to keep youuu in there with him."

Ava instinctively felt for her power, hoping to call up an underground river to wash the circus away. But there was nothing. Her magic really was gone.

Vivienne Morderay laughed as she saw them realize, then turned to go, the light reflecting off the jewels on her snake necklace.

And all at once Ava remembered.

"Wait!" she shouted. "Wait-wait-wait!"

Vivienne paused, regarding her coldly as Ava fumbled with the pockets of her cactus dress. It had been there all this time, ever since her own ride in the Wicked Wagon, and she had completely forgotten.

"Is this what you lost?" she asked.

With trembling fingers, she held up the sparkling topaz pin.

Shock exploded across the wicked witch's face.

"Mine!" she screamed, hurling herself toward Ava and shoving a hand through the bars. "Mine! Give it! Now!"

Ava began to jump back, then stopped as she noticed

something odd. Vivienne Morderay was close enough to seize the pin . . . but she hadn't. On a hunch, Ava lifted it, almost touching the witch's palm, but Vivienne couldn't seem to make her grasping fingers close.

"You can't take it from me, can you?" Ava said. "I have to give it to you."

Vivienne hissed, and for a moment her eyes turned black. But she didn't say anything.

"Well, in that case," said Ava, relief flooding through her, "I have some demands."

Gern gave a muffled chuckle. Henry and Crow looked at Ava with hope in their eyes.

"First," said Ava, "I want you to free all of us from this cage."

Vivienne Morderay glared, but she waved a hand and the cage vanished like smoke.

"Woo-hoo!" cheered Crow.

"Next, I want you to free Gern and promise to never trap him or any other gargoyle ever again."

The witch's expression could have cracked stone, but she muttered a spell under her breath and Gern's chains and gag melted away.

"Ahh," he roared, shaking out his enormous stone wings. "That's bet'er! Me gravel was really startin' to ache."

"Do you promise?" said Ava.

"I promise," Vivienne growled, her eyes glued to the jeweled pin. "Anything else, youuu greedy girl?"

Ava turned to her friends. "Boys?"

Henry blinked. "Um, I'd like a brooch that protects me from all biting and stinging insects, please." The others stared at him. "What?" he said. "I worry."

"I'd love some plorange cotton candy," said Crow.

"And I want a little magic mirror so I can talk to my family no matter where I am," added Ava. She turned to Gern. "How about you?"

"A new hat would be grand!"

The woman threw up her hands. "Who do youuu think I am? The Wizard?"

"I thought you were the great Vivienne Morderay," said Crow.

"And the feared Vivienne Morderay," said Henry.

"And the adored Vivienne Morderay," said Ava.

"Oh, shut up," said Vivienne Morderay. She jumped up and down four times, and suddenly Henry was wearing a sparkly green brooch, Crow was holding an enormous cloud of fuchsia cotton candy, Gern was wearing a dapper stone top hat, and Ava felt something heavy drop into her pocket. Checking it, she found a small gold mirror shaped like a snake biting its tail.

"That's enough now," said Vivienne Morderay. "Youu've made your trade."

"Fine, deal," Ava said, not wanting to push her luck. She held out the pin, hoping very, very hard this was just about a favorite piece of jewelry and she wasn't doing something she would regret.

Vivienne snatched the pin like a striking desert viper. "At last!" she cried. "After all these decades, the Lost Collar of Arboc is complete!"

She raised the pin toward her necklace, then stopped, her eyes flicking to Ava. "Where did youuu find this, anyway?"

"Stuck in the floorboards of the Wicked Wagon," answered Ava. "So that's proof Gern didn't steal it from you. You must have just dropped it on the way to school."

Too late, Ava remembered what Gern had told them about keeping their Swickwit connection secret. Vivienne's eyes blazed.

"Oho! *Not* good witches after all. Youuu know about the wagon, and youuu know the gargly-goyle's name. Wicked little witches!" She stared them up and down. "But how are youuu out of schooool? No getting out of Swickwit." She licked her lips, and even though she and her friends were free, and they had their magic back, and Gern was beside her, Ava felt a deep shiver of fear.

"I sense mysteries," Vivienne went on. "Oh yes. Why would youuu want to leave the best schoool in Oz? And how did youuu do it? So many mysteries." She locked her eyes on Ava. "Youuu will be hearing from me again, little girl."

Ava clenched her hands in her dress, wishing she'd asked for a few more promises before handing over the pin.

But it was too late. Vivienne was raising the topaz, her eyes full of a fierce, wild joy as she slotted it into the gap in her necklace. It clicked smoothly into place.

For a moment nothing happened.

Then Vivienne Morderay laughed. It was the same horrible, booming laugh from before, but now it thundered with triumph as black and purple lines of power crackled over her. Ava had never seen anything like it, not even when Crow performed Bone Fire. The laughter grew and grew, and Vivienne rose up in a cloud of flickering light, and as Ava and her friends watched, the carts and stands and banners and flags and even the big top itself were uprooted, rushing through the air into that light. The whole circus came collapsing down, becoming part of the flickering mass of power, and the laughing went on and on and on . . .

"Youuu will see me again!" Vivienne Morderay's voice

roared from the center of it all. "I am not throoouuuuugh with youuuuuu!"

And then, all at once, it was over.

Ava, Henry, Crow, and Gern stood on the grass of an open field under the clear blue morning sky. The sun shone on the Yellow Brick Road. Birds sang. A butterfly settled on Gern's new hat. There was no sign the circus had ever been there.

Warring emotions raged inside Ava.

On one hand, she couldn't help being deeply impressed by Vivienne. Wicked or not, the woman had more strength, style, and confidence than Ava had ever seen in one grown-up before, and if things were different, she would have wanted to become exactly like her.

On the other hand, Vivienne was famously very, very evil. Ava had a sinking feeling she would regret handing that topaz over for a long, long time. Completing the Lost Collar of Arboc had made Vivienne Morderay far too happy.

"Well," said Crow, smiling brightly as he wiped cotton candy off his chin, "I may not have much brains, but I think that went pretty darn great!"

29

THE FLIGHT HOME

"Great?" Ava said to Crow. "You think that went *great*?! What about me accidentally helping one of Oz's wickedest witches become even more powerful?"

"Or me knocking Crow into the cage so we all got trapped?" said Henry.

"Or me gettin' meself caught in th' firs' place," said Gern. "Let it go, you three. Viv's gone; she'll be a worry fer another day." He groaned, stretching out his wings again and kicking his powerful wolf legs in the grass. "Well, some 'oliday this turned out t' be!"

"How long were you trapped in there?" Crow asked.

"Almos' a month! But s'over now. What I want ter know now that we're safe"—he crossed his arms and frowned down at them—"is what ye three little 'uns are doin' not in school. How'd yeh get out?"

Ava hesitated, considering coming up with another lie, but Gern wasn't a teacher or anything—he was actually the nicest grown-up she'd met at Swickwit. She trusted him.

Quickly, she related their story.

Gern shook his head when she was done. "Never 'eard anythin' like it. I *should* take yeh all right back to Swickwit, but—BUT," he said, over Ava, Henry, and Crow's objections, "yeh did just save me from that cage."

"So you won't turn us in?" Ava double-checked.

"Wouldn't be right," said Gern. "I 'ope you three 'preciate it, though."

They all thanked him so enthusiastically Ava swore she saw his stone cheeks blush.

Gern nodded over at the ruined half of the Yellow Brick Road and its mess of spongy, tumbled bricks.

"An' yer sure that'll fix itself?" he asked. "Heaps o' Oz folks count on this road fer their liveli'ood."

"Oh sure we're sure," said Crow. "Ava said so."

"And her family grows bricks," added Henry. "So she would know."

Gern raised one stone eyebrow at Ava. "Yeh really reckon it'll be back t' normal soon?"

Ava swallowed hard. Fudging the truth to Gern somehow felt way worse than fudging the truth to the boys. But she was in too deep to back out now.

"It should be," she said, nodding and trying to ignore the hollow feeling inside her. "Once it dries all the way out, I mean."

To her relief, Crow raised his hand.

"Can I ask a question, Gern? Why didn't you want us telling that circus lady we were from Swickwit?"

The gargoyle sighed. "Well, that's goin' back a bit. I knew Vivienne Morderay as a student. Viv, she was then. A fierce little 'un, fierce as they come, an' powerful. An' always angry about the missin' bit from that necklace. If ye ask me, though, it was never 'ers in the firs' place. Stolen, tha's what I think. Anyway, I didn't want 'er knowin' yeh'd escaped the school. She tried a few times, see. Knew she'd be interested in ye if she found out you succeeded. Very interested."

"And now she knows," said Crow.

"Because I told her," Ava groaned.

"And she promised she's not through with us," finished Henry.

A gust of wind swept over them, dislodging the butterfly from Gern's hat.

"Well, ferget 'er fer now," the gargoyle said. "Fancy a lift where yer goin'?"

"Huh?" said Henry.

"I'm headin' back to Swickwit, but I think I heard ye three were goin' to WOW 'cademy?"

"Yes," said Ava. "We are . . ."

Gern waved a thumb over his shoulder. "Then 'op on. It's not far. I can 'ave ye there in 'alf an hour."

The three of them beamed.

"Really?"

"Wow!"

"Thanks!"

Relief flooded through Ava. For a minute there back in the cage, she'd been almost certain all was lost. But they were going to make it. The very final leg of their escape from the School for Wicked Witches was beginning.

One by one, they clambered up onto Gern's stone back. It definitely wasn't comfortable, with the spiky stone wolf hair poking into their legs and the huge wings whooshing on either side of them, but they weren't about to complain. They hung on tight as Gern leapt into the air, leaving the grasslands, the butterflies, and the Yellow Brick Road far below.

Ava's first realization was that Gern could fly much faster when he wasn't pulling the Wicked Wagon. He rocketed across the sky, zooming over the plain and farms toward the glistening city. Ava had never seen a city from the air before, and she tried to take it all in, but almost before they'd reached it they were soaring past, heading for the line of mountains.

Dark clouds were gathering around the foothills, so Gern flew higher, carrying them up to where the air was thin and cold. Now Ava was looking down on jagged, snow-covered peaks poking out of dense purple thunderheads crackling with lighting.

The moment the mountains were behind them, Gern angled down.

"I'm goin' to stay low from here," he called over the wind and Henry's moans of fright. "Not 'bout ter risk capture again so soon!"

Down and down they soared, until they came swooping into a pretty little valley between two high, craggy hills. Sheep and goats wandered the slopes, nibbling grass and wildflowers.

Gern landed with surprising gentleness, and Crow and Ava slid off his back to the ground.

"Oi, 'Enry," Gern said. "You can let go now."

Henry opened one eye. "Are we dead?"

"No one's dead," laughed Gern. "But yer squeezin' me ribs somethin' awful."

Ava and Crow coaxed Henry down, and the three of them passed around snacks and water before hitching up their bags.

"Right," said Gern. "West Oz Witch 'cademy is jus' over them hills. Walk through that gap there, an' ye'll be able to see it." He gazed down at the three of them. "I sure 'ope yeh know what yer doin'. Sometimes the right choice can be diff'rent from what we expect."

"We definitely know what we're doing," said Ava firmly.

"Hmm. Well, 'ere." Gern reached into his mouth and tugged hard, pulling out three smooth chunks of stone.

"Um, thanks," Ava said as he tossed one to each of them. "What are these?"

"Gargoyle teeth. Oh, don' look like that; they grow right back!" Gern grinned, and sure enough, new stone teeth were sliding into place. "That's my thanks to ye all. If ye ever change yer mind about where ye are, or need a bit o' help, just put that in yer mouth an' say me name."

They thanked him, and with a final round of good-byes Gern returned to the air, the three tired but happy friends watching until he was gone.

Ava stretched her arms overhead, looking around the beautiful valley. A sheep bleated, then another. The air smelled like grass and buttercups. It was as unlike Swickwit as any place she could imagine.

"Well," she said. "We did it. From now on, everything is going to start going right."

"Hooray!" cheered Crow.

"Thank goodness," said Henry.

Ava led the way through the grass and grazing animals to the gap in the hills, unable to stop smiling. After all this time, the place she was supposed to be was right around the corner. She took the final few steps, Henry and Crow at her heels, and they all stopped dead together.

West Oz Witch Academy sat just down the slope of the hill. The morning light gleamed off the silver dome with its lacework of windows, balconies, and crystal ornaments. The gardens surrounding the school were almost fully recovered from Ava's disastrous magic test and well on their way to being beautiful again.

One thing, though, was distinctly different: The top of the dome was crowded with people. Even from a distance Ava recognized Professor Ploosh's bald head and Dean Waterwash's silver robes, along with what had to be the rest of the teachers, all of them arguing with two enormous giants looming over the school.

One giant was a woman, the other a man. They had white skin and red hair, wore fancy flared suits covered in frills and sashes and bows, and were, judging from the way they were shouting and waving their arms, very, very angry.

Ava gaped. Crow stared.

"Oh," Henry said. "Oh no." He looked over at his friends. His face was gray. He gulped. "It's my parents."

30

HENRY'S SECRET

"Your what?!" said Ava.

"Your parents?!" said Crow.

They looked back and forth from little Henry Buffle, short and small and shy, to the two towering giants roaring in the faces of the West Oz Witch Academy teachers.

Ava could only think of one thing to say. *"How?"*

Henry hugged his arms around himself. "It was a curse. Some wicked witch cursed me when I was a baby. My parents spent years trying to track the witch down or figure out a counter-curse, but nothing worked. Then it turned out I had magic, and they were so excited. They told me I had to become the best in my class at WOW and learn to fix myself."

"Whoa," said Crow. "They couldn't just roll with it? Being human-sized doesn't really seem like that bad a curse."

"My parents think it is!" said Henry. "All they care about is getting the curse reversed so I can become a 'proper' giant like them. But I like being like this, at least for now. I've never known anything else."

"Have you told them how you feel?" asked Ava. She was still reeling from the news that Henry was a giant, but having parents who wouldn't accept you was pretty serious, too.

Henry gave an unhappy laugh. "I've tried. They won't listen. Plus, there's a bigger problem: My parents are kind of, well, the giant king and queen."

"They're what?!" said Ava.

"King and queen?!" said Crow.

"Yeah . . ." Henry wouldn't meet their eyes. "I'm, um, you know, a prince."

Ava and Crow goggled at him.

"Then does that mean you'll . . ." began Crow.

". . . Be king of the giants one day?" finished Ava.

Henry nodded. "Can't you picture it?" he said, holding out his arms and attempting a smile. His eyes brimmed with tears.

"Oh, Henry," Ava said. "You'll be a great king."

"The best ever," said Crow. "Because you're super nice."

They looked away politely while Henry wiped his eyes.

"Wait." Ava snapped her fingers as a realization struck her. "*That's* why you didn't want to go through the void back at Swickwit!"

Henry nodded again. "That was really tough. Lifting the curse would have made my parents so, so happy. It would have fixed everything with them. But when the chance was right there, I realized I didn't *want* the curse lifted. I don't even think of it as a curse. It's just the way I am. Just me."

"Plus, wouldn't you have knocked over Nettle Tower if you'd suddenly gotten all tall inside it?" said Crow.

"Probably."

Crow patted Henry on the shoulder. "Then thanks for not doing that. I like you like this, anyway."

"Same!" said Ava. "You're you, and that's exactly perfect."

Over at the academy, the argument between Henry's parents and the teachers was growing louder. Henry's parents were accusing the school of losing their son and demanding they bring him back. Dean Waterwash and the rest were denying everything and saying he must have run away. If they were trying to calm the angry giants down, it wasn't working.

"We should probably, you know, stop them," said Crow.

"Yeah." Henry didn't look too happy about it. "I'm gonna be in so much trouble, though. With the dean *and* my parents."

"We've got your back," said Ava. "Obviously we can't tell anyone about Swickwit, but if we stick together, maybe we can keep the grown-ups from being *too* mad at any of us."

Hitching up their bags, they headed for the school.

They had just reached the edge of the gardens when the argument up on the dome took a turn for the worse. Crackles and flashes of light erupted from the roof, along with pops, bangs, and a sudden cloud of purple smoke.

Some of the teachers had started using spells.

"Oh no!" said Henry. "They have to stop! Using magic will just make them angrier!"

He was right. Henry's parents were shaking their fists, shouting about being attacked and insulted. The dean and Professor Ploosh began arguing with the other teachers as well as the giants, and the situation looked only moments away from getting seriously out of hand.

"Mom!" Henry shouted. "Dad! Stop! I'm right here!"

But there was no way anyone could hear him over the chaos above.

"We need to get you up there somehow," said Crow. "Could you grow your shoes high enough for them to see you?"

"I'd fall over before I even got close!" Henry wrung his hands as his father jabbed an enormous, angry finger at

WOW Academy, punching a hole right through the stone.

"Hang on," Ava said, looking around her at the gardens. "I think I might have an idea!"

The orderly beds were filling out again, crowding with roses and jasmine, irises and lilacs. Ava had destroyed it all once before, but she'd learned a thing or two since then, and maybe this time she could manage to do the opposite.

"Do you trust me?" she asked Henry.

"Y-yes?" he mumbled.

"Then hold tight."

Planting her feet, Ava reached out for her power. She was tired—she'd done more magic in the last twelve hours than the rest of her witch career put together— and there was every chance the garden might remember her and force another bitter struggle like the one she'd had with the river. But as she opened herself to the life all around, she felt a sudden surge of support. Plants, it turned out, only cared about the future, and every plant in that garden wanted the same thing she did: They wanted to grow. Fast.

Perfect.

Ava poured in her power and the gardens erupted, each of the trunks, vines, and flowers doubling, then tripling in size. Leaves and petals burst out everywhere, weaving through and around one another in a riot of green, purple, yellow, blue, red, pink, and white.

Ava directed all of it at Henry.

"Hey!" he cried as the plants began wrapping around his torso. "Why are they—oh!" Understanding filled his face as he was lifted off the ground, rising up and up in a growing column of flowers.

Ava could already feel her strength beginning to fade, but she pushed through it, drawing on more and more power to send Henry up as high as she could lift him. When he was level with the top of the school, she paused, gasping, and Henry took his cue.

"Mommm!" he hollered at the top of his lungs. "Daaaad! Stopppp!"

And they heard him.

Both giants stopped shouting. They turned. They saw the tower of flowers and the pink-haired boy sitting atop it.

"Henry!" they bellowed together.

It should have been a happy moment, but Henry's father had forgotten about the teachers. One giant arm swung wide as he reached out for his son, and Dean Waterwash was lifted into the air. For a single unending moment she hung suspended . . . then fell gracefully off the side of the school.

Time slowed to a stutter.

Ava watched Dean Waterwash go tumbling down the dome, arms and legs and silver robes spinning.

Why isn't she stopping herself? Ava wondered. *Why isn't she turning into a bird and flying to safety? Why isn't she using her magic?*

The answer hit her like a winter sandstorm: Dean Waterwash didn't know she was falling. Dean Waterwash had been knocked unconscious.

Ava's mind went blank. She was too tired, too spent. She couldn't think of a single thing to do.

But in that endless, awful moment Crow bopped her arm and shouted, "Henry! Use Henry!"

One blink, and Ava understood.

She'd thought she had nothing left to give, but she dug down deeper than she ever had before, scraping up the very last sparks of her magical strength, and flung it all at the plants holding Henry.

"Whoooa!" Henry yelled as the column curled over, racing Dean Waterwash toward the ground beneath the walls of the school.

Ava got him there just in time.

"Duck, Henry!" Crow screamed. "Duck!"

Henry looked up, gasped, and at the last possible second, ducked.

Dean Waterwash stopped falling. She hovered in the air, nose to nose with Henry in his cocoon of flowers. She opened her eyes. She blinked.

Then she boomeranged in a whoosh back to the top of the dome, settling with a thump amid the crowd of terrified teachers.

There was a long moment of shocked silence.

Then the cheering began.

31

THE GREATEST MOMENT

Ava Heartstraw stared around her at the sparkling great hall of West Oz Witch Academy, feeling very, very proud.

And tired. She was so tired.

There hadn't been any time to rest after the exciting rescue of Dean Waterwash. First had come the reunion between Henry and his parents, which had involved equal amounts of relief and scolding that everyone couldn't help overhearing. Then the dean and teachers had flown down from the dome, surrounding Ava and Crow in the overgrown gardens, and for the next hour or so there had been just an awful lot of talking.

Henry rejoined the others before too long, and between them they managed to string together a story that seemed to have all the grown-ups (giant and otherwise) convinced. Basically, they said Henry had gone for a walk in the school gardens and seen a lost lamb from the next valley. When he tried to return it to its mother, he'd been kidnapped by Vivienne Morderay and her circus. Ava and Crow, who had been walking across Oz after escaping the School for Wicked Witches (because they were not wicked), had found Henry there and helped him escape.

There were plenty of holes in their story, but they literally couldn't tell the truth thanks to the Oath Scroll they'd left behind at Swickwit, and since Vivienne Morderay *had* captured them for a while, they felt reasonably okay about all the fudging.

The grown-ups had gone into a huddle after that, and the three friends had been whisked inside the school, where they were fed and cleaned up and gushed over. Everyone had already heard how they'd saved Dean Waterwash, and the staff kept having to shoo away curious crowds of gawking students and even some of the teachers.

Finally, they had received a summons to the great hall. And here they were.

Ava gazed around at the beautiful space, so happy to be back she was sure she must be glowing. The clear crystal columns and the shining star lamps were exactly as she remembered. The marble benches rising on either side were filled with silver-robed students just like before, and the platform with two throne-like chairs sat in front.

Okay, so maybe none of it was quite as impressive as it had been on her first visit. She wasn't a wide-eyed, small-town girl anymore, and when it came to sheer impact,

WOW Academy couldn't hold a candle to the dark glamour of Swickwit.

A faint tracery of scratches around the nearest column caught Ava's eye, and she smiled, recognizing the marks of her monstrous juicy-pop tree. Apparently, even magic hadn't been able to totally repair what she'd done that day.

The memory of those wild few minutes rose up in her. She'd been so hopeful, so excited and eager and certain. She'd had no idea how much her life was about to be turned upside down.

Well, she'd made it all the way back, and there was one big difference this time: She had friends at her side. True friends.

Crow was observing their surroundings calmly, looking very out of place in his green Nettle uniform. Henry fidgeted with his silver tie and avoided looking at his parents, who were peering in through the hole his father had poked in the roof.

Whispering from the benches caught Ava's ear, and she looked over to see Sheridan Gracefeather Montstable-Jones and her friends eyeing Henry and giggling. Ava suspected they might find him a whole lot more interesting now that they knew he was a cursed giant. Not to mention a prince.

With a pop, Dean Waterwash and Professor Ploosh appeared on the platform just as they had all those weeks before. The dean called for silence, and a pleasant anticipation filled the air.

"Welcome!" Dean Waterwash declared, her deep voice soaring through the hall. "We are gathered today to acknowledge the intelligence, courage, and goodness of three very impressive young people. Thanks to them, I am still here among you, and a potentially awkward diplomatic situation with the giants has been avoided." She gave a little bow to Henry's parents, who did not bow back.

"With that in mind," Dean Waterwash continued, "we have decided to present special awards to these three heroes for services to the school. Please step forward, Crow Backpatch!"

Crow turned red as the whole room filled with applause. He stepped up to the platform, rubbing his neck.

"Mr. Backpatch," said Professor Ploosh, his voice just as wobbly as ever. "In honor of your intelligence and quick thinking in a moment of crisis, we present you with this award."

The applause returned as Professor Ploosh handed Crow a plaque.

Crow raised his free hand, and the applause died away.

"Um, yes?" said Professor Ploosh.

"Yeah, thanks so much," said Crow. "But what quick thinking are you talking about?"

Professor Ploosh frowned. "I gathered from Miss Heartstraw's account of the events in the garden that it was your notion to deploy Mr. Buffle in order to utilize his unique anti-gravitational attributes."

"Huh?" said Crow.

"He means you told me to use Henry for his duck-and-return," called Ava.

"Ohh." Crow brightened. "I guess that was kinda smart, huh?"

"It certainly was, Mr. Backpatch," said Dean Waterwash. "It made all the difference in the world."

Ava had never seen Crow look as happy as he did walking back across the hall, and her heart swelled with pride for her friend.

"What's the award like?" she asked as he reached her. Crow held up a wooden oval, painted gold, with *Special Award: WOW* written on it in fancy letters.

Ava was a little disappointed.

"Henry Buffle, please come forward," called Professor Ploosh.

This time there was murmuring all around the hall. Crow was a stranger, so nobody had been more than politely interested in him, but Henry had been a student at WOW Academy for weeks. Now he was back after a mysterious disappearance with strange friends at his side, giants who said they were his parents, and, apparently, a royal title. He was getting a whole new start.

"Mr. Buffle," said Professor Ploosh as Henry approached the platform. "In recognition of your extraordinary bravery and willingness to put yourself in harm's way, we present you with this award." He held out another gold plaque, then paused. "That's in reference to you waving around on top of the flower tower and letting yourself be dropped directly under the falling dean, in case that wasn't clear."

Henry nodded. "I got it."

Henry didn't look quite as delighted as Crow as he walked back toward them, but Ava saw a tiny proud smile hovering around his face.

"Ava Heartstraw, please come forward!"

Ava got even more whispering and muttering than Henry. She kept her head high as she walked, the Wicked Witch of West Oz, finally returning home. She knew things now that would curl the hair of every student in this hall. She'd seen and done things none of them could even imagine. She'd faced dangers and villains and monsters and all sorts of frights.

She still felt a bit nervous, though. It turned out a whole crowd of kids watching your every move was always going to be nerve-racking.

"Miss Heartstraw," said Professor Ploosh. "In recognition of your extraordinary application of good magic for the sake of our school, we present you with this award."

Ava accepted her plaque, which was exactly like the others, as heavy chatter filled the hall along with the applause.

She was turning to go when Dean Waterwash got to her feet, looking happier than Ava had ever seen her.

"One moment!" Dean Waterwash commanded, quieting the crowd. "It is my duty now to issue one final thing today, and that is an apology. This is not something I am in the habit of doing, but in this case, it is very much warranted. So, Miss Heartstraw, on behalf of myself and all the faculty of West Oz Witch Academy, I apologize. I am sorry. I misjudged your magic out of my own ignorance of desert matters, and while I believe the mistake was understandable given the scale of the damage you caused, it was still wrong. *I* was wrong." She gazed around at the watching crowd. "Therefore, I am delighted to announce that Ava Heartstraw is not now, and never has been, wicked, which means I will no longer be named alongside Dean Phyllis Prancypants in the history books, and Miss Heartstraw is welcomed back immediately to WOW Academy!"

Noise filled the hall, and Ava felt her world sliding back into place as relief and pride rang through her. *She* had made this happen. She had clung to her certainty about where she truly belonged. She had worked and struggled for weeks and weeks, first with Tinabella, then with the boys. She had never given up.

It was the greatest moment of her life.

"Of course," Dean Waterwash went on, raising a hand to gesture toward Henry, "we are overjoyed to welcome back our own dear Mr. Buffle as well."

The giants watching through the hole in the roof boomed their approval, clapping so hard one of the windows cracked.

"And since West Oz Witch Academy is where mistakes are mended," the dean continued, magically magnifying her voice over the hubbub, "we are proud to offer Mr. Crow Backpatch, clearly the victim of false accusations by my East Oz colleagues, a place here among us as well."

Professor Ploosh's eyebrows shot up in surprise at this, but Ava thought she understood. Dean Waterwash cared more about her reputation than anything else. She would take any opportunity to make herself look good.

Ava's heart danced with happiness as she ran to throw her arms around the others. She had been accepted back! And the boys with her! It was everything they'd hoped for. After all their planning, all the dangers and struggles they'd faced together on the road, she and her friends were finally exactly where they belonged.

32

THE RIGHT CHOICE

"And for our final stop," said the prim older girl who'd been showing Ava around WOW Academy all evening, "this will be your bedroom."

She held the door open, waving Ava into a plain, narrow cell. It contained one small bed with gray sheets, one desk, one hard wooden chair, one empty shelf, and one square window looking out toward the hills.

"Wait, don't we have roommates here?" Ava asked, blinking.

The girl looked shocked. "Roommates? At magic school? Goodness, no! Can you imagine how distracting that would be? It would completely interfere with your studies."

Ava set down her bags and opened a closet beside the desk. Inside were five sets of silver robes, shirts, and ties. She ran a hand down them, waiting to feel happy and excited at finally achieving the uniform she'd been dreaming of.

It didn't happen.

It had been a dizzying afternoon.

Once the celebrating was over and the students back in their classes, Ava, Crow, and Henry had waited on one of the great hall benches while the dean and teachers had a long talk with Henry's parents. There was plenty of apologizing on both sides, but Ava was almost certain she'd spotted a triumphant gleam in Dean Waterwash's eyes when it was all finished.

Henry's parents had insisted on meeting Ava and Crow as part of saying goodbye, and there had been a great deal of hand shaking as they were thanked again and again for looking out for their son. Ava's shoulder still felt a little loose.

With the giants gone, Dean Waterwash and Professor Ploosh had escorted the three of them to the dean's familiar office, and the part of the day Ava had been dreading most had begun.

Somehow, though, everything had turned out okay. Ava suspected it had more to do with keeping Henry's parents happy than any goodwill on the dean's part, but all three of them were formally cleared to start classes as WOW Academy students. Even Crow, who baffled both grown-ups by answering honestly that, yes, he'd been starting his third year at the School for Wicked Witches and, no, he hadn't done one single bit of magic while he was there and couldn't show them any now.

In the end, Crow had been given a full schedule of remedial classes and led away by an unsmiling fifth-year boy to learn his way around the school. Henry, after successfully demonstrating a few of his new spell skills, had been sent straight to his old dorm room to start catching up on all the homework he'd missed.

As for Ava, Dean Waterwash had insisted on multiple demonstrations of her water control before declaring herself satisfied that Ava would not be destroying the school again, then sent her to wait in the hallway while an appropriate student guide could be found.

Ava had felt a little uneasy at how quickly she and the boys had been separated, but there was nothing she could do about that, so she'd used the wait to contact her family with the magic mirror from Vivienne Morderay.

The connection had been very confusing at first, as apparently a terrifying, ghostly image of her head had appeared floating in a bowl of pepper-root soup in her family home. Everyone but her mother had been busy in the brick moss fields, but once the two of them got things sorted out, they had a good chat.

Well, her mother had seemed to enjoy it, anyway.

Ava's family, it turned out, was thriving. The brick moss was doing well, and they were all enjoying having a little more food and room now she was gone. None of them had known she'd been ruled wicked and sent away, as they hadn't bothered to open any of the letters from

WOW Academy. Her mother said it was very nice that Ava was back, and she was sure she would make lots of friends and do very well and of course she'd never been wicked to start with and what a silly mistake the school had made. She hadn't really seemed to hear the rest of Ava's news, and had gone on for quite a while about the small successes and minor mishaps of Ava's eleven brothers and sisters.

As for Peaches, he had made friends with a three-legged dune fox and didn't appear to be missing her in the least. Everyone was doing just fine.

Ava had felt very peculiar when she closed the mirror.

Her family's world began and ended with the desert, and they were happy with it, but hers had grown over the past weeks. Grown a lot.

Sitting back in her chair in the silent, shining hallway, she'd begun to truly understand what that meant.

"So, do you have any other questions?" asked the girl as Ava shut the closet door.

Ava did have questions, plenty, and she didn't much like the answers when she got them.

It turned out WOW Academy classes were held from seven in the morning to seven at night. The food was simple, basic, and always the same. "To keep us focused on our studies," said the girl. Free time was overseen by teachers. There were regular very important tests. Only fourth-year students and above were allowed in the library.

Ava couldn't help thinking of how things had been back at Swickwit. She imagined her room in Nettle Tower, cozy and comforting even after Tinabella turned wicked. She thought of the chatter over breakfast in the Round Room and the uproar in the ballroom every night. She remembered the chaotic enthusiasm of Professor Mulch's classes, the den she and the boys had built under their library table, and the joy of the long, free afternoons.

"Are you all right?" the prim girl asked. "Your nose is running."

Ava blinked. "Yes!" She sniffed and wiped her eyes. "It's probably dust."

"Not at WOW Academy, it's not." The girl looked offended. "We clean the entire school every other day."

"Oh," Ava said weakly. "Great."

At last the girl left, and Ava flopped onto the bed, staring up at the ceiling and finally letting the worry that had been growing all afternoon wash over her.

West Oz Witch Academy was not like she had expected. Not at *all*.

Ever since her first short visit, she'd been picturing the school as a glamorous haven of magical opportunity and encouragement where she could become the best, most powerful version of herself.

Seen from the inside, though, it was more like a factory dedicated to strictness and conformity and control.

Ava felt downright tricked.

She did have to admit it might have been the tiniest bit her fault. She should have known appearances could be deceiving by now. Her own desert home seemed harsh and dangerous but was overflowing with beauty if you knew how to look. Swickwit kept its students safe by hiding behind a mask, literally disguising itself when outsiders were around. Even Crow concealed his once-in-a-century power, and no one meeting Henry would ever suspect he was both a giant and a prince.

Maybe nothing was exactly like it seemed from the outside. Maybe everyone had layers of stories underneath. Maybe she should have known all along that WOW Academy wouldn't live up to her dreams.

It was still a massive disappointment, though.

Ava's vision went watery, and she got up, hoping to distract herself by unpacking her bags. But she only managed to pull out her sky-blue spell book before she sank back onto the bed and surrendered to weeks of held-back tears as everything she'd been through came pouring out.

Her adventure wasn't supposed to end like this. Her life wasn't supposed to feel like this.

She'd repaired the mistake. Fixed the injustice. Forced her way back to where she belonged. After all that hard work, wasn't she supposed to be happy?

All she'd ever wanted was to prove herself. First to her family, then to WOW Academy, Warden Pike, Tinabella, Crow and Henry, and maybe even some of the mean kids as well.

But did proving yourself matter if this was how you felt at the end?

What did she truly want, right now, just for her?

Ava sniffed. She hated how crying made her nose all runny. Wiping her eyes, she pulled in a deep, shaky breath.

She'd chosen once. She could choose again.

She got to her feet, staring out her tiny window at the stars blooming in the West Oz night.

At least she wouldn't be starting from scratch this time. She had two good friends now, a decent amount of magic, and everything she'd brought in her bags. The boys would help. They might even come with her.

"Okay, I did it," Ava said, looking around her room on her very first day as a student at West Oz Witch Academy. "I'm here. Now how in Oz am I going to get back to Swickwit?"

ACKNOWLEDGMENTS

Books, like magic schools, take a crowd of people to make them happen, and that means I've got some serious thanking to do.

First thanks go to my team at Scholastic, starting with my editor, David Levithan, for championing this project and coaxing me patiently through the rockier bits. Thanks also to designer Maeve Norton, copy editor Starr Baer, and behind-the-scenes heroes Melissa Schirmer and Jalen Garcia-Hall. Truly magical thanks go to Teo Skaffa for the cover of my witchiest dreams.

Eternal thanks to my brilliant agent, Brent Taylor, and everyone at Triada US Literary Agency. I'm so grateful to be part of your team.

More thanks go to my family; to Grant Alexander for putting up with my rants about Oz; to Steven Carter-Bailey for the unending encouragement (quesos!); to Travis for keeping my heart warm; to Kurt for being a treasure; to Levi Hastings for the creative solidarity; to my entire Seattle writing community for the support and friendship; to Carleton Starr for the unending sweetness and patience; to Merlin for being a very good dog, even when you're not; to Amber for always; to Kate Bush and

Ursula K. Le Guin for being everything I ever want to be; to L. Frank Baum, for creating an enduring world millions of readers have loved getting lost in; and to Alex Kahler/ K.R. Alexander for being my best writing friend for over a decade and still putting up with me.

And thanks to you, dear reader. You are the reason I do this.

ABOUT THE AUTHOR

WILL TAYLOR cast his first spell when he was ten and has yet to be carried off by a dragon, so it seems to have worked. He is a reader, writer, and honeybee fan, and lives in downtown Seattle surrounded by all the seagulls and not quite too many teacups. When not writing, he can be found searching for the perfect bakery, talking to trees in parks, and completely losing his cool when he meets longhaired dachshunds.

His books include *The Language of Seabirds*, *Catch That Dog!*, *Slimed* (writing as Liam Gray), *Maggie & Abby's Neverending Pillow Fort*, and *Maggie & Abby and the Shipwreck Treehouse*.

You can visit him online at willtaylorbooks.com.